IDIOTS & angels

IDIOTS & angels

Sam V.K. Willson

To order additional copies of this book, contact:
Xlibris Corporation
1-888-795-4274
www.Xlibris.com
Orders@Xlibris.com
41725

CONTENTS

To

GSR

who makes all things right.

BAD DOG

When he set off that afternoon, with Butch on a leash, Joey Sindler knew how it felt to walk the last mile. He had seen death-house dramas on TV. He was thirteen, but since his father had died, Mom had no time to supervise his tube time.

He grew up with Flash, a pedigreed German shepherd that was two years old when Joey was born. Flash was a member of the family as if he had been Joey's older brother, stronger and braver than any brother would have been. When he died, Joey begged his mother for another dog. He never expected to find another Flash. And besides, his mother was not ready to pay the six hundred dollars that Flash had cost.

She and Joey watched the newspaper for any dogs for sale. But as the saying goes, Vermonters don't buy their dogs, they have them.

So one sunny Sunday afternoon, they decided to drive out of town and look for a dog for sale at some farm. Right on the outskirts of Pittsford, they saw a dog tied to a stake in front of a run-down farmhouse. When they slowed down, the dog began to bark and lunged to the very end of the long rope around its neck. It was fully grown but only half the size of Flash, grayish brown, bushy tailed, and with a noticeably wolflike head. His barking grew angrier, showing lots of teeth, when Joey and his mother got out of the car. An old woman came out onto the porch.

"Sometimes he gets sort of snappy," the woman said, standing on the edge of the porch. "But that's not why I'm selling him. My daughter wants me to come live in Worcester, and they won't take dogs. I think twenty-five dollars is about right. He's two years old."

"Very fair," Mrs. Sindler said. "May we get to know him a little?"

"Sure. Just be sort of careful at first."

Joey was already walking across the grass to the dog. "What's his name?" he called over his shoulder.

"We called him Butch," the woman said.

Hearing his name, the dog looked toward her.

Joey held out his hand. "Hi, Butch," he said. The dog turned to Joey and walked carefully toward him. Joey stood still, his hand extended. Butch approached and gently turned his head, inviting a scratch behind the ears. Joey obliged. His mother watched.

"Looks like we've got a new dog," she said and dug the money out of her purse.

**

A week later, she said to Joey, "We've got to get rid of that dog. Sorry, but it's just got to be."

Joey understood. Butch loved to roughhouse with Joey, loved to race around the yard after an old tennis ball. He leapt up as high as Joey's chest when Joey was getting a biscuit out of the cupboard. And when Joey went to bed at night, Butch sat next to the bed so that Joey could scratch his ears, and then scrambled under the bed and stayed quiet until Joey got up in the morning.

But Joey could never figure out why Butch couldn't get along with his mother, why he seemed to hate her. If she walked into the kitchen while the dog was eating his supper, he would look up, bare his teeth, and growl. If she walked into Joey's bedroom while her son was still in bed, Butch would claw his way out from under the bed, snarl, and bare his teeth.

"But, Mom, he never bites you. I think he's just scared of you."

"Why? Just tell me why."

"I wish I knew. I wish he'd tell me." Joey held Butch's new collar. As soon as the dog felt Joey's hand, he calmed down, usually lay down, and stared at Mrs. Sindler.

"Joey, listen to me." She was ready to leave for work. Joey was eating his cereal. "You know I'd feel terrible passing Butch off to somebody else. He could be dangerous. What if he bit some child? You wouldn't want that, would you?"

"No."

"And I'm always afraid he'll bite me."

"But he hasn't."

"I don't want to wait until he does. That would be pretty stupid, wouldn't it?"

"I guess."

"So we've got to have him put to sleep."

"You mean killed?" Joey felt the pain building up in his chest.

"Dr. Hassler will do it. It won't hurt Butch. It's just got to be."

"But he loves me. And I love him. We can't just kill him."

"I live here too, you know," she said. "I'm sorry. I'll call up Dr. Hassler and tell him you're coming with Butch this afternoon. It's a nice day, and you'll have a good walk."

"I can't do that." Joey felt he was going to cry for the first time since his father died.

"You're the man of the house," Mrs. Sindler said. "And he's your dog. You picked him out. We've made a mistake. Now we've got to correct it." She stood up and kissed Joey on the top of his head. "I'll call Dr. Hassler from the store."

**

Dr. Hassler's veterinary practice was in three rooms at the back of his house, which stood at the top of a steep driveway, in a heavily wooded part of town, with no neighbors within shouting distance.

His assistant, a middle-aged woman with a kindly face, came into the waiting room when she heard the bell jingle as Joey opened the door.

"Dr. Hassler wants to talk to you," she said. "He'll just be a minute. What's the dog's name?"

"Butch," Joey said. He was determined not to cry.

Along with the smells of medicine and antiseptic, Joey could smell something that reminded him of the time lightning struck a tree on their neighbor's property. It wasn't the smell of smoke, and Joey had never smelled another burning thing that smelled that way. It smelled of lightning, of electricity, and it got down in your lungs and made you stop what you were doing. Joey knew why brave men ran from the golf course when lightning was forecast.

Joey could smell electricity in that room. Butch was going to be electrocuted. If Butch smelled it, he would know what was coming. Joey closed his eyes and gritted his teeth.

"Hi, young Mr. Sindler. I'm Dr. Hassler. And this is Butch?" The veterinarian was big, gray haired, and smiling, a Santa Claus out of costume. He extended his hand to Joey.

Butch lay still on the floor. Joey thanked his lucky stars the dog had tolerated the doctor's approach.

"He looks like a healthy dog," Dr. Hassler said. "Is he pretty healthy?"

"Yes. But we've only had him a week."

"Your mother says he's a little snippy."

"Yes. Toward her. Not toward me."

"And," the doctor said, "not toward me either. May I hold the leash a minute?"

Joey passed over the leash. Butch stood up and looked up at Dr. Hassler. He stood stock still.

Dr. Hassler said, "It seems to me he's pretty well trained. Funny the way he reacts to your mother." He turned to his assistant, who was standing in the doorway. "Come over here a minute, Jane. I want to see how the dog—it's Butch, isn't it?—responds to you."

The woman took the leash from the doctor. Butch sniffed at her leg then looked back at Joey.

The doctor said, "I guess he doesn't hate all women. Too bad about your mother." He took the leash back and sat down next to Joey as his assistant retired into the back rooms. "I have a suggestion," he said.

Joey stroked Butch's back. "Yes, sir?" He dreaded what was coming.

"I have a friend, an old buddy of mine, down in Manchester, who's looking for a dog. He had a mutt like this forever, and he wants another. What would you say to my giving him a call and telling him I've found just the dog he's looking for?"

For the third time that day, Joey pressed his lips together to keep from crying, but this time for joy. "Sounds good to me," he managed to say.

"I'll keep Butch here until I can make contact. That is, if you don't mind. Of course, I won't charge your mother anything. Just tell her I said hello. I bet she misses that old shepherd you had. Flash, wasn't it?"

"I guess she does. But she's pretty busy."

The doctor stood up. "Well, I'm glad this worked out. I'll give my friend a call." He tightened his hold on the leash and led Butch toward the back rooms. Right at the doorway, Butch stopped and looked back at Joey.

Joey said, "No problem, Butch. Be a good boy."

The door closed behind them. Joey hoped his mother would be happy with the news.

BULL BOYNTON

"Well, he's certainly smart enough," he said.

"Too smart, I'd say."

"Don't forget, he went to Yale."

"That's what he says."

The men picked up their coffee cups, as if on cue, and sipped slowly. They were the six members of Rockford's Chamber of Commerce. They'd been doing well. For that matter, the whole town had been doing well. When the twenty-first century arrived, the six stores, two churches, and 1,800 residents of Rockford were a generally contented bunch of Vermonters.

"I guess you'd say he's handsome."

"You go ahead and say it. I don't think that's important."

"Important? Why isn't it important?"

"Bonnie thinks it's important. So she says. And he's real charming and wants to be accepted. She thinks we're acting too Yankee."

Bonnie was the daughter of Bull Boynton. She was in her late twenties, a waitress at Bill's Country Store, which was basically a restaurant, though they sold some parkas and blankets during the ski season. Also during foliage change. She had stayed in school all the way through Arlington County Regional High School. Not the smartest girl in the class, she didn't win any academic prizes, but she was probably the most popular and was actually voted Ms. Bundle of Cheer.

"I'm just saying what she says to me."

Winston "Bull" Boynton achieved the title of "Bull" by working, for thirty-one years (so far) at Collins Farmers' Market, lifting sacks of grain, and hoisting tillers into the back of pickup trucks, grunting ominously at anyone offering help. He was still called "Bull" by old friends or Mr. Boynton by the store's younger men when he became senior assistant, then associate manager. He drove a high and mighty SUV. Also, he was a deputy sheriff with the Arlington County police, which had the village of Rockford on its list of protectorates. His brother, Willy, was the full-time sheriff.

Bull remembered a call from Willy back in the late nineties. "Yes, indeed I'm mad, Bull. What the hell's this all about?" Willy asked.

"He was in a no-parking, he was drunk, and he gave me a lot of shit," said Bull.

"So?"

"So I straightened him out."

"We're being sued, you know."

"We were in the right, dammit. OK, so I got a little rough."

"Were you drunk? Tell it to me straight."

"I was stone-cold sober. I swear."

"Sober? I think you're more dangerous when you're sober. You should drink more. You're almost human when you drink."

He was sober at those midday meetings of the chamber of commerce, which made him edgy. Brother Willy was right. He was easier to get along with when he'd had a drink or two. Strange. He'd read that most men got angry and tough and beat up their wives when they were drunk. Bull knew that a drink calmed him down, let him love the world, and let him fall asleep early. At the chamber meeting, he was, unfortunately, sober.

"OK. You know what I think. It's my problem."

"Yeah, we know. You say he's smart, he's slick, he's going out with Bonnie, and—"

Bull interrupted. "OK. I'll say it. He's a dope dealer. A druggie." He'd heard it more than once, not only from the town gossips but from one of the bankers and from the Getty station, where he had a credit card that kept getting rejected. Then he'd pay cash. He always had cash.

The Congregational minister, an ex-officio member, said, "We're not sure about him, now are we?"

"Most of us are. Pretty sure. I'm pretty good at judging people." The chamber's chairman considered himself the resident expert on human nature.

"I think it's good to get proof before we go accusing somebody. How do we know? Nobody in town seems to have turned into a monster dope addict, not because of him. Maybe some of the ladies are using a little too much cough medicine, but—"

Bull said, "I just hope to God Bonnie knows what she's doing."

"Is it serious?" The chairman wanted to hear the latest news.

"She says they're engaged. She's a little afraid of ending up an old maid, if you know what I mean. And she says it's none of my business. She's twenty-eight."

"Better an old maid than a dope dealer's widow."

"She's sure he's not."

"Well, I'll say it before you do. Love is blind."

The newcomer had been in town a little over a year. His name was Ty Benson. He worked as a real estate agent with Green Mountain Properties. He said he moved to Vermont "because I was thirty and sick and tired of all those Boston snobs I grew up with." After college, he'd gone to work in the office of a national pizza chain and was lucky not to get fat. "Turned out I had an allergy to mozzarella cheese. Luckiest thing that ever happened to me." Most people agreed he was handsome and likeable and probably pretty smart. He rented a couple of rooms over the drug store.

It turned out he had visited Rockford three or four times to find out what jobs might be available. Drove up in his little red VW. He had a Massachusetts real estate license, for which he'd studied, secretly, while still with Pioneer Pizza. That license was transferable to Vermont. Green Mountain Properties was willing to hire another affiliate. Since his income depended on his sales, he spent almost every day out of the office. Nobody reported seeing him making the rounds. But a Rockford woman who'd gone on a shopping trip to Boston reported seeing him, or his twin brother, big as life on Tremont Street.

Bull Boynton tried to think objectively of his daughter. To understand her. It was hard to do. She looked so much like her mother, God bless her, that just looking at her made Bull feel bad. He'd been a widower for ten years—cancer—and prayed every Sunday, sometimes more, that it wouldn't pass down to Bonnie. As for her life, he wished she could do something more professional than waiting on tables. Maybe be a receptionist for a doctor in Woodstock or Rutland. Or study up on teaching kindergarten.

"I'm making almost as much as you, Daddy-o," she said whenever he suggested something other than waiting tables. Then she'd hug him, and he'd back off, and the subject wouldn't come up again for another month or so.

Everybody told him how pretty she was. Dark haired like her mother, and blue eyed like her father. Only five-two, like her mother, but strong, like her father. And her years waiting tables for locals as well as tourists had taught her how to be pleasant to everybody, a quality her father certainly did not possess. Her pleasantness as well as her looks made Bull think of his wife. So for his own peace of mind, he didn't spend a lot of time with her. She managed to keep the house, right on the little park in the middle of Rockford, decently clean and stocked with food. And she was in charge of the household finances. She and Bull had a joint account, and she deposited both of their paychecks and saw to it that Bull had enough cash in his pocket. She also made sure there was enough booze in the house for her father, not that she encouraged his drinking, but he enjoyed it, and she liked knowing that he could relax after hard work at the store. She herself only drank socially, which meant she hardly drank at all.

She also knew, as did Uncle Willy, that Bull was a different person when he drank. When Ty's VW arrived too early to pick her up before Bull had a drink, there were scenes she wanted to forget.

"You check with me, girl," Bull shouted, "before running off in the middle of the night. Hear?"

"Daddy, it's six o'clock. We're just going for a ride."

"I know who's going to do the riding, if that's what you want to call it. God, your mother would be ashamed."

Bonnie and Ty would leave. Bull would have a couple of whiskies and a chicken leg and be in bed by eight-thirty. But in the morning he'd remember. Those memories did not make him happy.

Bull only heard from his brother, the sheriff, very early in the morning or in the evening after work. Perhaps a ski meet requested a couple of uniforms to keep the tourists in line. Or the fair at Topham needed traffic control since it was the busiest weekend of the Topham year. There were plenty of deputies on call for those daytime duties. Bull heard from his brother when something was planned for after dark, like a church supper there in Rockford. The sheriff thought it was good PR to support the churches. His men could appear to be, perhaps, religiously inclined, with specially appointed parking attendants, which might benefit Willy's chances for reelection. And the deputies always got a fine supper.

On a warm August day, Bull got a call from his brother at two in the afternoon.

"Can you get away for an hour or so?"

"Sure, I suppose so," Bull said. "Why? I'm in no mood for a wild goose chase."

"I'm double-parked right outside. We can go out on the highway for a cup of coffee. I'll pay."

"Gee, I can't wait," Bull said. "What a treat! Coffee!"

"Shit, you can have whatever you want, asshole."

Bull got into the county car. He could smell his brother's aftershave. He'd get Bonnie to buy him a bottle of whatever it was. He was tired and sweaty, and Willie was looking crisp as could be. The contrast did not improve Bull's state of mind.

Over coffee, Willie said, "We've got some interesting information. I wanted you to know about it first."

"First? Ahead of who?"

"Just shut up. I got a call from New York. They say there's going to be a big drop tonight at the quarry."

"What the hell's a big drop?"

"A shipment of crack. Maybe some heroin."

"Right in the middle of our pretty little park?" Bull said.

"Sure, idiot. Like I said, at the quarry."

"Ah, the old quarry."

"They say we're about halfway between Boston and Montreal, so the guys from Boston can drop it off here, and the guys from Montreal can pick it up and take it home."

"Sounds like a spy movie."

"The access road off the highway is usually deserted at night. The quarry closes at six. New York says it's a typical drop-off point."

"I always thought they exchanged evil things on park benches."

"They say this is not just a rumor. And I have a little problem."

"Like?"

"I'm supposed to be in Bennington tonight for a sheriffs' convention. Giving a speech."

"So?"

"So do you want to play big-time cop? Just find the package, and you'll be a hero. You might even get your picture in the paper. Irresistible?"

"Just search around the quarry? What if I got shot?"

"Then you'd definitely be a hero."

"Hooray."

"New York knows all about the quarry. Of course, they didn't tell me they were up here, the bastards. They found a natural drop-off place just left of the gate. In the wall. Apparently been used before. In that old pile of broken marble."

"Stuff falls down into the quarry and gets lost, or the company has to send divers for it. I know all about it. That hole is as deep as a twenty-storey building. Half the size of a football field and full of water."

"Yeah. Well, you're not going inside the gate. It's locked at six. All you have to do is poke around in the old wall and find the package."

"Promise I'll be a hero?"

"And listen, Bull. Don't drink. Stay sober. Wait till the job's over. And there's some really bad news here, brother." He had saved the worst news till last. "New York says your son-in-law, Benson, is involved."

"My son-in-law in a pig's ear!"

"And you'll love this. He has a wife in Montreal. Drops in on her every month or so. The drug scene heats up right after he's been there. Montreal's ready to arrest the wife."

"For shit's sake!" Bull took a deep breath. "Just tell me what time to be there. In your professional opinion."

"New York says the stuff should be there by ten. So wait until midnight, right? We're not supposed to catch the bastards. New York says they'll handle the arrests."

"Always the bridesmaids, never the bride."

"Sorry about all this, Bull." He tried to sound businesslike.

"Hey, it's no skin off my ass. Not one bit. Why don't you just take me back to work?"

That afternoon, Bull felt like he was functioning in a nightmare. He was dead tired when he finally left the store. At home, the golden brown whiskey looked better than ever, but he had more or less promised not to drink. Bonnie was already home, her bedroom door shut, which meant she wanted to take a nap. Bull made himself a frozen dinner, chipped beef on toast, and had a glass of Coke. He hoped that his kitchen noise would wake Bonnie up, but no such luck.

It was eight-thirty when he finished reading the newspaper. He wasn't supposed to go up to the quarry till midnight. Or was it ten? If he had to stay at home until midnight, he'd probably fall asleep and not wake up until dawn. That would not be good.

What if he caught the bastards? He figured he should be wearing his uniform. Bonnie had had it cleaned since the last church supper. The door to her room was still closed. He was glad she didn't know what time he was leaving. He wanted to tell Willy he'd followed instructions.

It was dark when he got to the quarry entrance. The driveway down to the gate was about a hundred feet long. Heavy woods on each side. He drove down to the gate, just to remind himself of the place. He hadn't been there in years. He was slightly surprised to find the gate open and a light burning in the one-storey building where tools were kept and, he imagined, dynamite.

And divers probably put on their rubber suits in there. He was tempted to leave his car at the gate and go check on the light. But he wasn't supposed to be there until midnight, so he backed up almost to the road and backed his SUV into the underbrush, next to some low-growing hemlocks that hid him from the road. He wondered if the people in the little building had heard him. But no one appeared.

He wasn't sleepy. He was mad at his brother for handing him all this shit without giving him time to . . . well, maybe get ready for it. One minute he was sorry Bonnie was sleeping when he got home, but the next minute he knew he'd have an awful time facing her with all this crap. Then he thought the people at the quarry should be reprimanded for leaving the gate open and the lights on, but who the hell gave a damn? He would have given a week's pay for a single shot of booze.

So the smart-ass New Yorkers were right. They had figured that not a single car would be using the road before ten. Still, Bull had no trouble staying awake. Finally, he heard something coming along. About time! It turned into the driveway, its headlights on full. Just after turning in, probably when it spotted the lights in the quarry building, it turned off its lights.

And Bull saw it was a red VW.

No soldier who had a hand grenade thrown into his foxhole could have moved faster, more purposefully, almost hysterically. The key was in the ignition. He jerked the SUV through the underbrush. He turned on his lights. The VW was almost to the gate. Bull was going forty. He didn't stop. He slammed into the back of the VW and kept going. Kept pushing. Pushing.

The VW was too shocked to steer toward the building. Without a sound, it sailed into the quarry. There was a noise like a single crack of lightning when it smacked into the water.

Bull braked just short of the edge. He waited for someone to come out of the building. When no one came, he backed up the driveway. He was panting as if he'd run down that driveway and personally, alone, pushed the VW into the quarry. It never crossed his mind to look for a packet of dope. He had killed the bastard.

No one came out of the quarry building because no one was inside. The light had been left on and the gate open by a workman who had things other than quarry safety on his mind.

Divers went in two days later, to measure the depth of the water and figure how long it would take to pump it out. They found the red VW. It had two passengers, Ty Benson and Bonnie Boynton.

Bull never admitted his involvement, and his brother never asked. But at the end of the year, Bull quit his job and moved away. He asked the post office to hold his mail. After a year, they sent it all to his brother. Bull never showed up again.

A BIG NEW WORD

I didn't officially attend the party. I was in my midteens, so a New Year's blast was still off limits for me. Mom and Dad sent out invitations a month in advance. They still had money in those first years of the Depression. Dad had been lucky on the stock market, and Mom kept the household budget within reason. I don't think they were showing off with the party. They've always struck me as being genuinely friendly people. They had a thousand friends . . . well, perhaps fifty there in Brattleboro. They also had the nicest house on the street, and it seemed built to give parties.

Trying to stay hidden in the shadows at the top of the stairs, I watched people arrive that New Year's Eve, the women in long dresses, some of the men wearing tuxes. The good spirits they were in when they arrived soon became even better. The music was loud. The waiters, who came with the caterers, hustled around. I wished I'd been twenty-one instead of fifteen.

I remember that Mom looked like that lady in the Chas Addams cartoons. All in black, a high collar, some sort of sparkler at her throat. Of course, her hair didn't straggle down like in the cartoons. Mom was really beautiful. I've told her she reminded me that night of the witchy Addams lady. She laughed her head off.

All the crystal bowls Mom and Dad had inherited were out on the dining-room table. I think there was lobster salad and roast beef and probably a whole turkey, smoked. At least we were eating a lot of turkey sandwiches the next couple of days. And very expensive champagne was served, according to Mom. It must have tasted darn good. When I was helping clean up, I counted forty-two bottles. And half the women claimed they didn't drink. Maybe they made an exception for New Year's Eve.

A couple of screams from downstairs got me out of bed just before midnight. A pair of candles on the mantle in the living room had fallen over, and Mrs. Porter, who I've always thought was a little squirrelly, figured the house would burn down. Actually, the candles left not a single mark.

That year, Mr. and Mrs. Seely gave the party on New Year's Day. It didn't start until late in the afternoon, giving people time to recover from our party. Pretty much the same people, I assumed, though of course I wasn't invited. But I heard a lot about it. Mom estimated there were a hundred roses in the Seely's living room and dining room. Dad reported he'd asked Sylvia Seely about her necklace, and she confessed it was brand new. Diamonds. Twenty-five thousand dollars worth of diamonds. Dad wasn't much into jewelry, but that necklace impressed him.

"Interesting," he said at supper a couple of days later. "I didn't know the gas company was doing so well."

Mom said, "Anyway, they don't tie the president's salary to the company's earnings, do they?"

Dad said, "Of course not. That only happens . . . if it happens . . . on Wall Street, not in Vermont."

Mr. Walter Seely was President of Vermont Gas and Electric, a company that had been around, as far as I know, since the beginning of time. Their offices on Main Street had a nice white marble front and big brass doors. When I sometimes went into the office to pay the bill by hand, I was very wary of the slippery tiled floor. Once I'd seen an old lady fall. I think Mr. Seely himself helped take her to the hospital.

When I reported the accident to Mom, she said, "He's the kindest man in town. You know, he put up the money to start the pet hospital. And he gives a lot to our church. That's probably why they keep electing him to the vestry."

I knew that Mom and Mr. Seely had been in high school at the same time and dated, though Mom said they never went steady. He had been a good baseball player, usually second base I think. More than once, it crossed my mind that Mom still had a slight crush on him. He was certainly handsome. Dad described him as a black Irishman, whatever that meant.

Mom claimed Mrs. Seely was the biggest spendthrift in town. "Those roses were in bad taste. Impressive, but it wasn't a funeral. Right in character for Sylvia."

"Does she play golf?" Dad asked. "I can't remember."

"Never," Mom said. "Belongs to the club, you know, but claims her doctor advised her not to play. Supposed to have a bad back. But of course she doesn't miss a party up there. The drinks are big."

"Is she a drinker?"

"Does the sun come up in the morning? Don't act naive, love. You know she drinks."

Mom always looked nice, but Mrs. Seely could have been a model. In those days, we boys and men wore suits (my first nonknickers suit) and ties to church, and the women wore hats. Families always sat in their ancestral pews, our family pew having been inhabited by my great-grandfather, Zeke. It was really Ezekiel, but they called him Zeke. And maybe even some ancestor before Zeke had that pew.

I happen to know how the Seelys got their pew in the second row on the left. Old Mrs. Considine died and didn't have any children. To hear my parents talk, the pew had barely cooled off from Ms. Considine's rear end before the Seelys claimed it. Sylvia Seely's Sunday hats could therefore be seen by everybody in church. There just happened to be a large sunny window right at the end of that pew. Mom pointed it out. Nice coincidence for Sylvia Seely's hats.

The Seelys' daughter, Jan, was a couple of years behind me in school. She was beautiful and very smart. I remember she finally graduated as valedictorian of her class. But her main claim to fame was as the editor of the school paper. She wrote highly moral editorials that Mom suspected her mother wrote for her. And she spoke French at the drop of a hat, or should I say chapeau? For six weeks every summer, she went to Camp LaBelle in Maine, the most expensive camp in New England, where the young ladies learned horseback riding, gourmet cooking, and French verbs. My parents decided the scout camp in Benson would be the best place for me.

**

When the awful news came out, I learned a new word. Nobody discussed it, at least not in public, but there were significant glances and eyes rolling up when the subject seemed ready to surface. My new word was *embezzlement*, which meant robbery. It was impossible to imagine Mr. Seely robbing anybody, let alone his own gas company where he was president, so people called it embezzlement. I never learned all the details, but I know he pleaded guilty, had to pay back ten thousand dollars, and went to jail for a year and a day. And he actually did go to jail, up in Windsor. It was hard to imagine.

Mrs. Seely's life changed very little. She still came to our house when it was Mom's turn to entertain the bridge ladies. She and her daughter, Jan, were in church every Sunday. I noticed she didn't stop to talk after church the way she used to. And Jan only wrote an editorial once a month instead of every week. Life, in fact, kept going along, just as normal as ever, with a great deal of silence about the biggest scandal in Brattleboro's history.

What did I learn? Well, people try to keep things on track, even after a bridge has washed out, as Dad used to say. And they are kind to the victims, at least to their faces. In fact, sometimes they're kinder than they were before.

I also learned that a hundred roses are too many.

And I've always remembered what *embezzlement* means.

NATIONAL DOG STAMP

Boys will be boys, particularly when they're twins, eighteen, smart, and full of the devil. Not to mention when they're Vermonters, determined, and dog lovers. These twins were named Bob and Ben, and nobody (except perhaps for their mother) was entirely sure which was which. They were high school seniors, lived with their long-suffering parents on Grove Street, an upscale neighborhood, and were considered by most people to be lighthearted troublemakers. One time, for instance, they were leaders of a posse of half a dozen boys who managed to hide the big bass drum of the Burlington marching band just before a crucial football game. Burlington nevertheless won, but the afternoon was remembered as a victory for Fairmont High.

Their father, Emory Simpson, who was the oldest teller at Fairmont's Vermont National Bank, was usually apologetic about his sons, automatically defensive even when they won a prize at the Vermont state debating competition (the only two-person sibling team in competition,) or came in second in Fairmont County tennis doubles. Mr. Simpson was so accustomed to hearing bad news whenever his sons' names came up that he couldn't help dejectedly shaking his head whether informed of a victory or some new deviltry.

Their mother, Maude Simpson, had lost control of her sons so long ago she now felt like a distant relative, loved but seldom considered in the decision-making process.

Three houses down the street from the Simpsons was another big Victorian property owned by Paul Fulton. He was retired from the railroad (an office worker), stout, bald, and what was then called a "confirmed" bachelor, a sad, not a complimentary, label. (In the '50s, it never crossed anyone's mind that a lifelong bachelor could be anything but sexless and pathetic.) And he was famously stingy, never putting more than a dollar in the plate on Sunday except for Easter, when he gave five dollars carefully earmarked for flowers, preferably lilies.

As far as the Simpson twins were concerned, Mr. Fulton had one redeeming feature, his dog Flash, a handsome five-year-old German shepherd. When Flash arrived as a puppy, the boys regularly stopped by after school to play with the dog. And the custom continued year after year. Mr. Fulton had fenced in his backyard but made a wire gate that may have been intended to let the boys in to see Flash without their traipsing through the house. Fairmont in the spring and fall was muddy, in the winter icy and muddy. The house's back door, opening into the fenced backyard, was never locked. Nor was the house's front door. Nobody in Fairmont could remember a burglary ever taking place.

When the U.S. Postal Service announced its campaign to find a suitable dog for an eight-cent stamp, the twins instantly thought of Flash. No handsomer dog existed. No friendlier one either. But to their amazement, old Mr. Fulton wouldn't think of entering him.

"I don't believe in an eight-cent stamp," he announced. "What good's an eight-center? It falls right between the hay and the grass. And I suspect it would be yellow, like the present one. Flash wouldn't look good in yellow. Anyhow, he licks himself enough as it is. He doesn't need millions of people licking his stamp."

The postal service had eight huge vans traveling around the country in search of the ideal canine. The van assigned to New England was painted with the service's big blue eagle on a snow-white background. Big letters proclaimed the Dog Search. When it got to Fairmont, it parked in front of the railroad station. Apparently, everybody in town planned to enter a dog. They flocked to the big van, studied its broad steps in the back leading into the body of the vehicle, the low pedestal inside for little pooches to sit on, and the oriental rug for reclining large dogs. Several lights and a huge camera were visible.

The town's excitement was shared by the twins. Flash had to be entered. Flash would become immortal. Flash would live in every stamp collector's album. What if Flash were offered a movie contract? Look at Lassie. Or Toto. Or someone might write a book about him, like *The Hound of the Baskervilles*. Or make a statue like the one in Edinbrough of the dog who couldn't be cajoled away from his master's grave. No, the Simpson twins wanted no fame for themselves, only for Flash, and of course for Flash's owner, stubborn, stingy old Mr. Fulton, who was apparently unaware of the worldwide fame that might lie ahead of him.

The twins' plan turned out to be beautifully simple. Ben (or perhaps it was Bob) put a handkerchief across the mouthpiece of the telephone. He'd read it was a sure way to disguise your voice and called Mr. Fulton.

"Sir, you've been selected by the Wallingford Farmers' Cooperative to receive one of our special high-return savings accounts, the 9 percent account." Ben spoke slowly, officially, the way he imagined a bank's loan officer spoke.

Mr. Fulton, who had checked the banks all over the county for the highest-paying savings account remembered that the Wallingford Farmers normally paid 4 percent. "Did you say 9 percent?" he asked. "I thought you were paying four."

"That's right, sir. But our founding fathers did not intend the cooperative to run at a profit. And to our surprise, we find that we have a bit saved up that must be disbursed. You understand, I'm sure."

"Well, I knew you were nonprofit."

"And we've chosen seven deserving families to make this offer to. Nine percent for an indefinite period."

"Well, I'll have to think about it."

"There's just one requirement, Mr. Fulton."

"I figured there'd be a fly in the ointment."

"Oh, no fly, sir. We just insist on meeting with you face to face for the signing of the papers. At your convenience of course. When would be good for you?"

"Well, Wallingford is thirty miles away. Maybe some afternoon. Now I'm retired, I don't get up too early."

"Excellent. What about Wednesday? Our chairman will be here on Wednesday, and I'm sure he'd want to meet you. You probably know his name. Mr. Avery MacIntosh? You specially chosen people will be very important for the bank, now and in the future."

"I guess Wednesday's OK. About three, three-thirty?"

"Perfect, sir. Wednesday the twenty-third. Here in our office. You do drive, don't you, sir? Or can we send a car for you?"

"No, I drive. All right. Three o'clock on Wednesday. Just one more thing. You did say 9 percent, didn't you?"

"Nine percent, Mr. Fulton. Rather incredible, isn't it?"

"OK. I'll be there on Wednesday. Avery MacIntosh, is it?

"Yes, sir. We look forward to meeting you."

**

On Wednesday, the boys waited in front of their house to watch for Mr. Fulton's car heading south toward Wallingford. After he had been gone for five minutes, they hurried to his backyard, hugged a leaping-for-joy Flash, and set off for the railroad station. No stage mother could have been more nervous than the twins. They found twenty or more dog owners in line ahead of them. Flash lifted his upper lip at a nasty-looking Jack Russell but otherwise seemed content to wait his turn. The twins plotted their next move.

It was five o'clock before Flash's moment came. The twins filled out the form with his vital statistics, explained that his owner was unexpectedly called out of town, and pushed Flash down onto the oriental rug. Flash loved the attention. His ears pricked up when the photographer held up a dog biscuit and said "Good boy." The flashbulbs made him jump to his feet, but by then his handsome head, perhaps about to become immortal, was engraved on film. The boys, confident they had a winner, led him triumphantly back toward Grove Street.

Mr. Fulton's visit to the Wallingford Farmers' Cooperative was somewhat less successful. He parked his Pontiac right in front of the building and went in at exactly the appointed time. There were no other customers at the moment. The single teller was counting bills, and a gray-haired, cosmetics-free woman sat at a desk, presumably a manager of some sort.

Mr. Fulton cleared his throat in front of her desk. She looked up from her spreadsheets and stared at him unsmilingly. He was clearly an interruption.

"I'm here to meet Avery MacIntosh," he said, trying to sound respectful but confident. He smiled.

"Avery MacIntosh?" the woman repeated.

"Yes. The president, right?"

"I have never, ever heard of an Avery MacIntosh. This is the Wallingford Farmers' Cooperative. We do not have a president. We are a cooperative. What sort of business did you think your Avery MacIntosh was in?" Her tone was as brutal as a third-grade teacher explaining to a student that Moscow was not, and never had been, the capital of France.

"Someone called to tell me about your 9 percent savings account." He began to suspect that he might not have won the lottery.

"My dear sir," she said, "who exactly called you?"

Mr. Fulton felt the blood brightening his face. "I didn't get a name. A man."

She patted the phone on her desk. "This is the only phone in this office. I'm the only one who occasionally calls a customer or supplier. We do not now and never have offered 9 percent. Never. Perhaps you dreamt this phone call."

Mr. Fulton nodded in the affirmative. "Yes, that must be it. Hard to understand. Sorry to bother you."

He started back for Fairmont at half past three. On his way, he stopped in Clarendon for a glass of sherry at the inn. Before he knew it, four-thirty sounded from the big clock on the mantle. Sun going down. Time to get on his way.

**

It was dark when the twins led Flash toward home. At Mr. Fulton's house, a light went on in an upstairs room, then went off, and then the next room's window lit up. The boys laughed out loud. Mr. Fulton was obviously still searching the house for Flash. He must have been searching ever since he got home. Time for the next step in the plot.

Ben led Flash through the gate into the backyard. Bob walked quietly up onto the front porch, counted to ten, and rang the bell.

Mr. Fulton, looking frazzled, came to the door. "Hello, Ben," he said. (He had a 50 percent chance of getting the name right.) "What can I do for you?"

"Gee, Mr. Fulton. I haven't seen Flash since I got back. I just wanted to say hello."

"You went away?"

"We both went to Chicago on a field trip for school. We studied meatpacking."

"I see. Sounds interesting. Well, Flash seems to have run away."

"Oh gosh. No. Flash wouldn't run away."

"I have looked under every bed, behind every door, in every closet, in the cellar, and in the attic. I have hollered his name 'till I'm hoarse and whistled till my lips froze up. He is not here."

"Shall I call?" Bob asked.

"Sure. Go ahead. He's gone."

When Ben, holding Flash on the back porch, heard Bob shout the dog's name, he quietly opened the back door and let the dog into the house.

Mr. Fulton said, "You see? He's gone."

"But look, sir," said Bob. "That's Flash right there." The dog came trotting down the hall toward Mr. Fulton.

"Oh my God. Oh my God. She's right. That woman at the co-op is right. I've been dreaming."

"She, sir?" asked Bob innocently.

"Never mind. Thank you. I don't understand . . . Good night. Thank you."

**

Mr. Fulton's doctor recommended that he go to the Mary Hitchcock Hospital in Hanover for a brain scan and general look-over. In the meantime, he should drink lots of water and try to get more exercise.

Two full years later, the twins had still not heard anything about the post office contest for America's most beautiful dog. In fact, by then they'd forgotten about the whole thing.

THE STAR OF DAVID

(In doing research for our book, *Holocaust Hell*, we heard about a lady in Brooklyn who was one of the few Jews from the Munich area who survived. She welcomed our visit, and as she recalled her experience, we asked if we could record her memories. She graciously agreed. Here is what she told us.)

I was eighteen in 1943. I had a boyfriend, but he had disappeared. I think he went to Switzerland. I worked with my brother in the jewelry store. He had inherited it from our father. It had been in the family a long time. Nothing too fancy, but it paid the bills.

My brother was twenty-five. His name was Josh. I remember him sitting most of the day at his workbench with a *loup*, you know, a magnifier, in his eye. He was always thin, no matter how much he ate, but you can see I get fat. We both had light hair; I wouldn't call it blond but almost. He was nice looking. He was always at his bench or behind the counter, but he kept his shoes shined. Father taught him that. And I tried to look nice. Nothing very fine, but decent. Sometimes Father let me wear a necklace or a bracelet from the store, and my brother let me do it too.

In 1935, our mother left. She was smarter than our father. She wanted to take us with her, but our father said no. She went to a cousin in Cuba who taught in a university. I'd like to visit them someday, but we've lost touch. She wrote to us sometimes. I still have her letters. I'll show them to you. But I don't think she was very happy there. She died almost exactly two years after she left. Our father said it was God's will. And then our father died. Also God's will I guess.

When the Nazis took men into the army, they never sent them back to their hometowns. Same for the Gestapo. The soldiers got sent off to the front, mostly Russia as I remember, and old men from other parts of the country came to run a town like ours. Not men as old as I am now, but certainly not young warriors. They didn't know anything about the town, not about us or any other citizens, just what they put together from what part of town we lived in and what they heard from gossip. What we looked like made a difference. They didn't bother us for a while because we were blond. But some Jews were being sent to work camps. They didn't exactly disappear, but they certainly didn't volunteer. You know what happened. Everybody got nervous. The Nazis took some people, but they didn't take others. You never could tell. Sometimes they came at night, a lot of banging on doors and people screaming. It must be hard for you to imagine.

Well, the day I'm talking about, three of them came into the shop. Middle-aged men. All of them in uniform, but I remember noticing that not one of them had any ribbons on his jacket. I wasn't sure if they were officers or just plain soldiers. They all wore helmets. The main one was short and fat. But he was not . . . how do you say, "jovial?" He looked like somebody's uncle, but he didn't smile or even say good morning.

The counters were L-shaped. I was standing at the end near the front window. My brother was at his bench at the other leg of the L. Of course, he stood up when the soldiers came in. But the Nazi in charge didn't go straight to my brother. He took a couple of steps into the shop, looked around, and then came straight to me. He told me to give him the necklace I was wearing. I tried to undo the clasp, but he reached up and yanked it right off my neck. I remember it hurt. He said thank you as he stuffed it in his pocket. I was too afraid to say anything.

He was carrying a picture of some sort, medium sized, I'd say about twice as big as a book. He muttered something to the other two soldiers. I couldn't hear, and they stood right at the door. Then he told my brother to come around the end of the counter. I knew my brother was trying to stay calm, to look relaxed, but I knew he was as scared as I was.

The Nazi stepped over to the wall and leaned his picture up against it. It was a needlepoint Star of David. Very colorful. Beautiful work. There was no glass over the front to cover the needlework. My Christian friends had handmade pieces like that in their homes. One I remember was called the Sacred Heart of Jesus. This Star of David was as beautiful as that. God knows where the Nazi got it.

Then he said something like "If you'll excuse me" and started to unbutton his pants, his fly. I sat on a stool behind the counter. I thought I was going to faint. I think my brother was just as horrified as I was. The Nazi urinated on the Star of David. He kept looking up at my brother, I suppose to see what effect he was having. And kept on urinating. As he buttoned up, he asked the other two soldiers if they needed to pee. They both shook their heads. I got the impression they were rather shocked.

My brother just stared at the Nazi. Then he began to tremble, just a little. Only once before had I seen him do that. The night our father died and my brother was with him. He kept a perfectly straight face. It was so straight it didn't look real. Didn't really look like him. Like some horrible mask. Maybe even a death mask. And the trembling got a little worse. Nothing he could do about it.

I couldn't see the Nazi's face, but when he spoke, it sounded like he was smiling.

"Oh dear, I think this man is sick. Look at him shake. Are you sick?"

My brother's jaw was clenched. His expression didn't change. He just stared at the Nazi.

"Perhaps he has some terrible sickness. We must find out. We must protect the town. We can't have sick people wandering around, now, can we? You understand."

He turned to the soldiers at the door. "I'm afraid he's too sick to walk. Come help him. Try not to touch any bare skin. He might be contaminated."

They didn't have to drag him. He walked. He looked at me. I suddenly realized I might never see him again. I was right.

The Nazi picked up the Star of David and shook off the wetness. He said, "This really is quite useful. Pretty, isn't it?"

(She asked us if that was the story we wanted. We thanked her and promised to send her the book. She insisted we stay for tea.)

SPLIT DECISION

"How nice hearing from you. How are you, Timmy?"

"Good."

"How's your dad?"

"He's good."

"So what's going on? I don't get a call from my favorite sixth-grader every day."

"Dad said you'd tell me a story."

"Now, which story is that?"

"He says you got bullied too, Grampa, and you'd tell me about it."

"Aha. You're getting bullied, are you?"

"This guy who lives down on Baxter Street, Chuck Perrin, bumps into me in the hall and jabs my side with his elbow. And he hits me in the shoulder. Sometimes it's black and blue. And he calls me a faggot."

"He's in your class, is he?"

"Yes."

"I bet you're smarter than he is."

"Maybe."

"So I guess I know the story your dad's thinking of. I got bullied once. I was probably in the sixth grade too. I don't think the word *faggot* existed way back then, but Harold Havens called me sissy, and I guess that was about the same as faggot. I was a helluva lot smarter than Harold, if I say so myself, and I suppose that ticked him off. But basically it was just fun for him to pick on me. Fun for him. I imagine your friend Perrin gets a kick out of it too."

"Maybe."

"It's hard for an idiot like that to imagine what a bastard he's being. You can't reason with him. Have you tried talking to him?"

"No, not really. What should I say?"

"It might not do any good. He'd just be glad to know how unhappy he makes you."

"I'm not too unhappy, Grampa. He just makes me mad."

"Well, good. So one day, I and the guy picking on me decided to have a fight after school. A fistfight. That kind of a fight can be really dangerous. I don't recommend it."

"Perrin would beat me up."

"Well, you never know. I'll tell you what happened to me. First, I've got to tell you about this guy in our class. He wasn't exactly retarded, if you know what I mean, but he was slow, real slow. He was two or three years older than the rest of us. Been held back a couple of grades. We were all bad, because we called him Dummy. He didn't seem to mind. I sort of liked him, big galoot. You know, the way you'd like a Saint Bernard. And I guess he knew I wasn't looking down my nose at him. Of course, I knew he was pretty dumb, but he was nice too.

"Well, anyway, about a dozen kids came to watch. Probably Perrin told them what a Mohamed Ali he was going to be. Some girls, too. Don't know why the girls came because he was homely as a clubfoot."

"What's a clubfoot, Grampa?"

"Well, that doesn't matter. Just take my word for it, that Perrin guy was no beauty. Of course, there wasn't an umpire or anything, or a gong, so there was a bit of hesitation at the start. But I pulled my arm back and aimed right for his face. And then you know what happened? Dummy was right behind him and threw his arms around him, holding Perrin's arms at his side. You get the picture?"

"Yes."

"Of course Perrin lurched forward, trying to get loose, so with my sock and his yanking himself forward, the collision was something to write home about. I hit him right on the side of his face. And you know what?"

"What?"

"I dislocated his jaw."

"Wow."

"And he fell down and clutched his jaw and started to yell like a banshee."

"Wow."

"And I just walked away. But that's not the end."

"What?"

"My hand was hurting like the devil. By the time I got home, it was really killing me. My mother soaked it in Epsom salts, but it kept getting worse. So that evening, she took me to our doctor, and you know what?"

"What?"

"I'd broken three little bones in my hand. I was in a cast for six weeks, with just my thumb and one finger sticking out so I could do my school work."

"Gosh, that sounds terrible. Did it get better?"

"Since that was about forty-five years ago, it has indeed gotten better. But I think your dad wants me to advise you to wear boxing gloves if you want to fight."

"I don't have boxing gloves."

"Then you better try negotiating. Or maybe that guy who's picking on you will just get bored or find somebody else to bully."

"I don't think he'll get bored."

"Well, Timmy, all I can say is try negotiating. It's hard to believe, but maybe what he needs is a friend."

"I don't want to be his friend."

"Hey, you never know when a friend's going to come in handy. Don't forget Dummy. You just never know, dear boy, you never know."

CONFESSION

She turned off the soap opera when she heard the knock at the door. She didn't mind missing the episode. She'd been napping for the last half hour. She knew that most of her neighbors too, there in the assisted-living home, Greensward Meadows, dozed in midafternoon.

The gray-haired man smiled and nodded when she opened the door. He was wearing a dark suit under a wrinkled old raincoat.

She said, "How do you do?"

He said, "My name is Ted Foerster. Class of '53. Long, long ago."

"Come in," she said. "My memory's not too bad, but I must admit . . ." She stared at him hard, trying to jog a memory. "Were you in our dorm?"

She and her husband had lived in the dormitory called Eliot Cottage for a quarter century. Ten senior boys a year. She remembered a surprising number of faces.

"No. I was in Lakeland. I've dropped by because I saw in the alumni magazine that you are now the senior faculty wife emerita, or whatever it's called."

"Isn't that something? Eighty-four years old, I've outlived everybody else, and I've smoked and drunk and never even considered jogging. Good old New England stock."

"Congratulations. It must really be wonderful."

She said, "Do sit down. Shall I put on some hot water, or shall we just reminisce without tea? I'm having a bit of sherry. Would you care for some?"

She was wearing a floor-length black velvet dress. Or was it a dressing gown? She looked rather regal with the pearl necklace against the velvet, her snow-white hair perfectly in place, the oval rimless glasses framing her blue eyes.

"No sherry, thank you. I'd love some, but these New Hampshire highway cops can smell liquor a mile away."

As they chatted, she commented on her contemporaries, the men who had taught her visitor, Ted Foerster, so many years before. And the coaches, special tutors, and librarians. Her memory of those days was fine. The school, St. Sebastian's, had been in existence a little more than a hundred years, and she and her husband had been there for more than thirty years, a good third of the school's lifetime.

"You know, my husband died ten years ago. Cancer. But he still told his great jokes right to the end. He told them so often they became a sort of school tradition."

"What a great way to be remembered. I knew he'd passed away."

"He said seventy-five years were plenty. I'm afraid I disagree with him more every day."

"I can't remember if you had children."

"I had a boy and a girl by my first marriage. Married at eighteen and divorced at twenty-one. George treated them as if they were his own. But as for more, we felt those two were enough."

Ted Foerster said, "I have a question for you I've been wanting to ask for about thirty years. It's bugged the hell out of me. And of course it bugged Tony, my brother, right up until he died. Believe it or not, it was just about the last thing we talked about."

She looked at him and cocked her head. "A question? If you need some old friend's address, you can get it up in the administration building. I gave up on my address book years ago. These days I can't read my own handwriting."

"It's about my brother. Remember him? Tony Foerster?"

She thought for a moment. Then her face, even her posture, seemed to stiffen. "I thought the name Foerster was familiar. Of course, I remember him. He lived in our house." She got up, went to the window, and closed the venetian blinds, even though it was a gray November day. She turned on a light next to the couch where Ted Foerster was sitting and sat down again in her high-backed chair.

Foerster said, "He lived in your dorm, yes. The first semester of his senior year, almost up until Christmas break. 1971."

"Yes," she said, a hint of coldness in her tone. "And what do you want to know?"

"Just one thing," he said. "Why did you say he made a pass at you?"

"Ah, I knew it. That's what you wanted to know." She stared at him, frowning and firm-lipped. "Because he did. That's why."

"And he was expelled from school. He told me he had to be gone in twenty-four hours."

"I don't remember the details," she said.

Foerster said, "He and I were very close. Not all brothers are. Even when he was in Hollywood, we talked on the phone, usually once a week. I'm godfather to both his children. And he asked me to be his executor. We had no secrets. None. He swore to me he never came on to you. Never made a pass. Never paid much attention to you."

"I'm afraid he wasn't telling the truth." She glanced at her watch. "Sorry."

"He said you were beautiful, the most glamorous faculty wife in the school. He said the boys used to kid about you, about where they'd like to take you on a honeymoon. But he never ever stepped an inch out of line with you."

"It's just not true. If that's all you wanted to know, I'm sure you have other things to do. Are you a journalist, Mr. Foerster?"

"No. Retired banker. First National."

She considered his answer for a moment. "Bankers have to be discreet, don't they?"

"Yes."

"But what about brothers? They can reveal things to anybody they want, right?"

"I guess they are not legally bound, but I've learned how to keep secrets. Tony told me things about Hollywood that were pretty horrendous, and I never thought of repeating them. Never."

She said with a faint smile, "He was a handsome boy. And confident, or should I say cocky? Captain of the soccer team, I remember."

"He was athletic all his life. Loved sports."

"And was plenty bright. Knew how to get ahead. How to succeed without really trying."

"Yes, it was quite a gift."

"George was very fond of him." She took off her glasses and made an elaborate production of wiping them, breathing on the lens, and wiping them again.

Finally, she said, "All right, Mr. Foerster. I suppose you deserve to know what happened. I hardly think it's the sort of thing I need to take to my grave. And it may make your life a little happier. That's a good motive, isn't it?"

"Yes, it is."

"I just ask you to keep it a secret. It won't benefit anyone else, and it would only destroy some fine reputations. Do you give me your word, Mr. Foerster?"

"Yes, I do."

She folded her hands in her lap and looked past him at nothing in particular.

"You know the stories about lifeboats with little hope of rescue, with too many survivors and too little water? Somebody has to be thrown off, or all the others will die. Sacrifice one to save the many. Do you know that story, Mr. Foerster?"

"Yes, I know it. I know variations of it."

"Then you'll understand what I did. Perhaps not approve, almost surely not approve, but I think you'll understand." She paused. Then, "You know what bisexuality is, of course."

"Yes."

"My husband was a bisexual. You know how I knew? Because he told me. Before we were married. I think he loved me, and I know I loved him, so we tried not to have any secrets. I had my two children, so I wasn't anxious to have any more. Sex wasn't ever terribly important for me. And in spite of his . . . well, his problem . . . he was in every way a wonderful man. Believe me."

"Actually, Tony talked mostly about you, not much about your husband."

"Tony married and had children, did he?"

"Three wives, three divorces, and two kids."

"Good for him. You see, for the first time after we married, after eighteen years, George fell in love with one of our boys. Tony obviously. A spectacular-looking boy, Mr. Foerster. In fact, spectacular in every way. But you know that." She took a sip of her sherry. "And how did I find out? I'm sure you want to know that."

"Yes, I suppose so."

"My husband's study was up on the third floor, away from the phone, available to any of the students who needed help. I'm glad you're not smiling, Mr. Foerster. For all those years he offered help and nothing else, I assure you. He had a desk and two chairs in his study and, of course, lots of books and a daybed when he wanted a catnap. He got tired like anybody else. He coached, you know, as well as taught. He was a very active man."

Ted Foerster nodded. He could only listen.

"One evening, his mother called. From Virginia. She was sobbing so hard I could barely understand. Her husband, George's father, was dying. He fell from a ladder and broke his spine. She had to talk to George. That minute, that very minute. He should come home. He ought to see his father.

So I walked up to George's study. He and Tony were on the daybed. I'll just say they were not napping. I went back downstairs and told his mother that George was out of the building. He'd call when he came back."

Ted Foerster said, "Tony never told me anything like that."

"Of course not. I don't blame him. But I had to do something. I had to save my husband, his job, his reputation, his . . . shall I say, his honor? He was an honorable man, Mr. Foerster, despite what you think."

"I'm not passing judgment. I'm just surprised."

"I knew that people would believe me. I knew the headmaster would. And the head of George's department. I knew that if I said Tony had made a pass at me, they'd never doubt it. And if Tony fought back by saying George molested him . . . don't you love that word *molested*? I doubt Tony ever felt molested . . . then it would sound like he was making up a story to contradict me. But people would believe me. I was sure they would. And they did."

"What did your husband think of all this?"

"He had to rush to his father in Virginia. Actually, people began to think Tony had made a pass at me after George left. That made my story even better. I asked the dean to get Tony out of the dorm as soon as possible. He was gone by the end of that next day. I'm sure you understand, I was fighting fire with fire."

"That's one way of looking at it."

"I never wanted to confront Tony. I'm sure he never confided in his friends. What could he say? My husband and I survived. His job here, his career, survived. He was an emotional wreck for a long time, supposedly over his father's death, but he pulled himself out of it. You know something interesting? More alumni sent letters to his good-bye dinner than any teacher had ever received before? It made him very proud."

"It's a wild story."

"True stories often are. I don't suppose there's anything else you want to know."

Ted Foerster stood up. "Thanks for trusting me. For telling me."

She smiled up at him. She said, "Please, stay and have a glass of sherry. Just a drop. Hand me one of those glasses. Don't they say confession is good for the soul? My soul is already feeling better."

He hadn't noticed it before, but she pulled the sherry bottle up from beside her chair.

"OK," he said. "Thanks." He held out his glass for her to fill. "Here's to the good old days," he said, and raised his glass to her.

THE DEATH OF BARBARA CZERNY

The death of Dan Czerny's wife made headlines on every New York paper. He and I had been good friends at Princeton, and even our wives seemed to like each other at our twenty-fifth reunion a couple of years ago. But I had not been in touch with him for a year or more before her death.

"Oh God, it's good to see you," Dan said. "Come on in. Come in. Come in."

They had lived for ten years or more in their big apartment on Riverside Drive, not far from Columbia, where Barbara taught and practiced clinical psychiatry. She also had a private practice at home. I had read a couple of her articles. They seemed practical, understandable to a man in the street like me. Dan was an editor at *Time,* mostly sports, an occasional article on the theater.

I said, as Dan pointed me toward the living room, "It's a ghastly situation, old buddy. We're all behind you. Just let us know if we can help."

"Oh, I'm OK. When you live through something like that, you either die on the spot or, as my mother used to say, rise above it. I'm a slow riser, but I'm not sinking either. I've just made a pot of coffee. Want some?"

Although coffee at eight o'clock at night usually gave me acute insomnia, I agreed. I sat on the couch, facing two big easy chairs, with the coffee table in front of me. The room was comfortable, not fashionable. No modernist interior designer had been near it. My mother would have been comfortable there. So was I. The hum of traffic from the drive was somehow reassuring. There was a big bouquet of roses on the Steinway. I wondered who had sent them.

Dan came in with our coffee. "Let me tell you one thing." He was trying to sound businesslike. "I didn't lie to the police."

"Nobody said you did, did they?"

"I didn't lie, but I didn't tell the whole truth. Those cops would have thought I was lying. Or had gone completely round the bend."

"Listen, kiddo," I said. "Just tell me what you want. Or don't tell me anything. I'm just here to listen, or if you want, I'll talk. Want to hear about IBM?"

"Let me talk for a while. If I get to a sticky place, you can tell me about life on Wall Street."

"You found her, didn't you?"

"Well, yes. You could say that. That was a Wednesday evening when she gave her adult education class. It lasts until nine-thirty or so. Right at Columbia. A five-minute walk."

"She came home alone?"

"Almost always. She was braver than Achilles. Sometimes somebody in the class wanted to spill his story out, and she was always sympathetic, always made time for him or her. But yes, usually she came home alone. I got home by ten-thirty. Wednesdays we put the magazine to bed. I'm never home early on Wednesdays. She had what was left of a glass of wine in front of her. But don't get me wrong. She wasn't a drinker. Just a glass now and then. Not a heavy drinker like most of these teachers around here. But she was very excited, dying to talk."

I said, "She was the soberest person, at the reunion."

"Exactly. So she came back from her class and rang for the elevator. When the door opened, there was a kid already in there. She thought he was about fifteen. Since he'd come down from an upper floor, she assumed he lived in the building, but she couldn't remember seeing him before. She said he was just a typical kid off the street, jeans, baseball cap, and a long bulky sweater. Of course, nothing frightens her. She said hello, and Jesus Christ, the kid pulled a gun on her."

"I'd have fainted dead away. The poor gal."

"A big silver-plated gun. She figured it had been hidden in his jeans. She said he started to mumble something about money, but you know what she did?"

"What, for God's sake?"

"She suggested he come up with her for a cup of coffee and some cookies."

"What guts!"

"And believe it or not, he said OK and stuffed the gun back into his pocket."

"What did she do? Hypnotize him?"

"I wish I knew. Can you believe her standing up to a gun that way?"

"What was the kid? Hispanic? Black?"

"She said he was probably Irish. Later on, she began to think he was Hispanic, but she said he looked slightly different every time she looked at him. 'Cloudy,' she said, 'and somehow radiant.' I guess a fifteen-year-old can look radiant, but cloudy?"

"What the hell does that mean?"

"You tell me. A radiant kid who sometimes looked cloudy. That's what she said. And she was right at the top of her form. You know, not a bit tired, very excited."

Dan's story fascinated me; all this radiance and cloudiness and silver-plated guns and mystery kids. I figured that even without the coffee I'd have lain awake all night after this story.

"Then somebody knocked on the door. She asked the boy to give her the gun, which he did without a complaint, and she put it in the drawer of that end table. Then she went down the hall to answer the door. The man was tall, white haired, and in a white suit. Not too many white suits around here in April, but she said he looked at ease. He said he'd come for the kid."

"Come for?"

"He said the boy had to come with him. 'And why is that?' she asked. 'Are you his father?' And the man said, 'I am not here to answer your questions, Mrs. Czerny. And I'm afraid you'll come to regret it if you argue with me.' By that time, the boy had come down the hall behind her. 'I'll go,' he said. 'Are you sure you want to?' Barbara said. The man in the white suit reached past her and took the boy's arm. 'I warned you not to argue. You should have listened, Mrs. Czerny. Perhaps we'll meet again. I think we should.'"

"Who was he?" I asked. "Who did she think he was?"

"She said he had the same slightly cloudy look as the boy. That's what she said. Cloudy."

"I wish I could picture what a cloudy person looks like."

Dan said, "Me too. Boy, do I wish it." He paused to take a sip of coffee. His hand was shaking. He put the cup down without lifting it to his mouth. "She went to see if the gun was still in the drawer. It was gone. She figured the boy must have taken it. Can you believe, in the middle of all that, she said to me, 'I hope he doesn't hurt himself. He was an awfully skinny kid to handle that huge gun.'"

I said, "Do you think skinny means cloudy?"

"I don't know. But she was a smart lady. She didn't say the man in the white suit was skinny. She said he was cloudy. Just like the boy was cloudy."

"I remember, don't worry. What time was all this, before you got home?"

"I got home a little after eleven. A half hour had gone by after the man and the boy left. She was much too excited to go to bed."

I said, "Do you want to tell me any more? You know I—"

"The police decided she'd had a massive heart attack."

"I read that in the paper. I guess it sometimes happens."

"She was sitting right in this chair where I'm sitting. I was on the couch where you are. Please believe me. This is the part I didn't tell the police."

"Of course I'll believe you."

"She had just finished telling me about the boy and the man when she suddenly looked up over my head at something behind the couch. Her eyes and mouth were both wide open. Naturally, I jumped up and looked. There was nothing there. Absolutely nothing. And then she started to choke. Her hands were up around her neck, no, an inch away from her neck as if she were trying to pull something away. Trying to pull something that was choking her. If hands had been there, that's what she'd have been doing. Trying to keep someone from strangling her."

"Oh my God!"

"But there was no one there. I tried to pull her hands away from her throat, but they had become like cast iron. Nobody could have pulled them away. And she was standing at a funny angle as if she were being held up by the neck."

"Oh God, Dan!"

"And then she just dropped to the floor, her hands beside her, normal-looking hands with two or three broken fingernails. I did mouth-to-mouth. I tried to pump her chest. All I could do finally was close her eyes. And call the police."

"Of course they never suspected you."

"Maybe a couple of them did. But there wasn't a single mark on her neck. Nothing at all. And when the coroner found the heart attack, that was all there was to it. The police have never called since."

"So did she choke on something?"

"She was just drinking a little red wine. She never choked in her life."

"So?"

"There was something she saw, something she knew, something I couldn't see. As close as I came to . . . well, participating, were those unbelievably strong hands around her neck, her hands. But not her hands. Not for a minute."

I stood up. "I'm flattered you told me all this." There was nothing more to say.

"Keep it to yourself," he said. "She's dead. That's all that matters."

"Yes, I guess so. Of course, I'll keep it to myself. I'm not sure that's all that matters, though."

"That's all that matters, I assure you."

"Again, thanks for confiding in me. I've got to run. But I think I'll take the stairs. I'll leave the elevator to others, braver others, like Barbara, I guess."

"Oh God, if she'd only given that kid a couple bucks."

I patted him on the shoulder. "Good night, kiddo," I said. "Lunch one of these days?"

"I'd love it," he said. "I think that's what she would have recommended."

"It's a deal," I said, and headed down the stairs.

ONE GOOD DEED

Peter was late for his trip to the city. And of course, the gallery would expect him to be on time. Everybody loved shaking hands with the artist. Little did they know of the fun artists made of their amateur admirers. But they spent the money, and Peter was glad they did.

As he was backing out of his driveway, he saw the LaMontagnes' stuff all over their scraggly front yard. Yard-sale time. They were good neighbors and presumably his friends. Originally from Quebec, a couple of generations back. Good Catholics, three kids in their teens, Dad a mechanic at Forsythe's Garage, Mom an occasional nurse's aid at the hospice.

Peter got out of his elderly Mercedes and waved to Albert LaMontagne. "Wow, I almost forgot. Gotta run, but had to take a quick gander." He hurried through the islands of junk.

On top of a card table, there were half a dozen little pictures fit for a child's room or a campy bathroom. Leaning against the table's legs were bigger paintings. Their frames bruised and faded, the paintings hard to see in the late afternoon light. As he glanced at them, Peter realized that Al LaMontagne was standing beside him.

"Glad we're getting this stuff out of the house. It either gets sold or tossed. What'll you have? Another guy sometimes buys these old pictures and scrapes the paint off. Says the canvas underneath is useable. You ever tried it?"

Peter shook his head. "It sounds like a good idea. But by the grace of God, I can still afford canvas, thank you." He pointed at one picture, propped up in front of his knees, in a rather fine frame. "Where did that one come from?"

"Crappy, isn't it? It was my grandmother's. I remember it from Montreal. It's yours for ten bucks."

Peter picked up the picture, slanting it into the light.

Al LaMontagne said, "You know, I've got to admit I've always hated that picture. Loved Grande-Mere, of course, but that picture stinks. Those water lilies or whatever they are seem to be at the wrong angle. They don't seem to be really floating. And who ever saw water that color? Is it blue or green or what? And that weird bridge looks ready to fall down in the next rainstorm. Hey, take it. I'll be glad it's out of the house."

Peter spotted the capital *M* followed by smaller harder-to-read letters in the lower right corner of the picture. It was about twelve by eighteen, doubtless a study for a larger painting.

If Peter had been a cartoon character instead of a forty-year-old painter, he would have had an angel sitting on one shoulder, a red devil on the other. They would both have been shouting into his ears. He would have heard, "For God's sake, tell him, or he'll never forgive you!" Simultaneously, he would have heard, "You're on the brink of fame and fortune. Leap, dammit, leap!"

He pulled ten dollars from his wallet. He was afraid Al could hear his breathing. He looked again at the painting. He was going to be financially independent for the rest of his life.

Then he remembered the gallery opening in the city. Now he was a good half hour late. He was damned if he'd leave that painting in his car, parked in Greenwich Village.

"Hold on to it over the weekend. I've got to go to town. OK? I'll pick it up on Monday."

Albert LaMontagne nodded. "No problem." He took the painting from Peter and set it back on the ground, leaning against the table leg, but this time the back of the painting faced out. It had been sold and would soon go back into the house.

On his way into the city, Peter let his jubilant imagination take charge. He hardly noticed the heavy traffic. He remembered a similar study at Monet's home in Giverny, occasionally displayed at Jeu de Pommes in Paris. Would a million dollars be too much? Hell, a million would only buy a fairly decent house in the Hamptons, with no ocean view. Better ask three million. Maybe if he gave it to NYU, they'd give him an honorary degree. Doctor of Fine Arts sounded nice, but it wouldn't pay for a Jaguar. He'd never get one of those national medals from President Bush. That guy wouldn't know a Monet from a Persian birdcage.

His arrival at the gallery was deemed fashionably late. A happier artist had seldom graced an opening. A little group of two women and a man argued quietly over which one would make a pass at him. Some of his tremendous good cheer communicated itself to the whole champagne-sipping room. One after another, the little red stickers, meaning "sold," started to appear.

Peter felt like kicking himself for making dinner plans for the evening. After dinner, there would be a bit of discreet clubbing, and he might eventually even find himself in a new and congenial bed. And then obligatory Sunday brunch at his sister's on Seventy-second Street.

He decided not to hang around the city after brunch. The LaMontagnes never went anywhere, so he'd be able to pick up the Monet that evening. The car radio was playing "Carmen." He whistled along. He would set the painting up on the table right beside his bed. Now, that would be something nice to wake up to.

He knocked on the LaMontagne door. He wanted to seem casual. Home earlier than expected, so why not take the picture off their hands. One of the sons came to the door.

"How you doing, buddy? I told your Dad I'd be home tomorrow, but my plans changed. He's holding a picture for me. Figured I'd pick it up tonight."

"He's down in the cellar," the young man said. "I'll tell him you're here."

Peter heard voices in the dining room. If he went in, he was afraid he'd get trapped for supper. He wanted to fly home with his prize in his arms.

Albert LaMontagne came along the hall, carrying the picture. "Hi," he said. "You know, we LaMontagnes always go the extra mile." He chuckled. "But this only took five minutes. Here you go."

He handed the picture to Peter. The paint had been scraped off the canvas. Peter prayed he was having a nightmare.

"Now you can paint one of your own on there. The canvas looks pretty sturdy, don't it? The paint just chipped right off, easy as pie."

Peter felt there was a large empty area where his heart and stomach used to be. It didn't cross his mind to speak, to scream, to smash the picture across Albert's face. Or say thank you. He felt light-headed. He turned away, walked across the porch, held on to the railing going down to the lawn, and went home.

Before he went in, he looked at the stained old canvas once again and dropped it into the garbage pail.

UNCLE LOU'S PROBLEM

"Listen," I said to Aunt Rosie, "Don't let him leave me the farm. I'm strictly a city boy."

"You know how he is," she said. "I don't have much say. But don't start worrying. He's still in pretty good shape."

Aunt Rosie and Uncle Lou were well along in their sixties. Uncle Lou may have been seventy. His family tree, which was also mine, could be traced back to the early 1700s, first in Massachusetts, finally in Vermont. Living outdoors most of their lives keeps people from looking their age. Some look older, and some look healthy and younger.

My aunt and uncle had no children. I was the only nephew that paid them much attention. It was easy for me. My job at MIT wasn't that far from Bennington. And besides, I liked them. I liked them a lot.

The farm was on the outskirts of Bennington, about a hundred acres, and in the family since just after the Revolution. Wonderfully fertile land with Otter Creek running through it and big stands of sugar maples on the edges of the fields. At planting and harvest time, Uncle Lou hired a couple of men to help, always the same two men as long as I could remember. During the long winters, he fiddled with his two tractors. Come spring, they were in fine working order.

Aunt Rosie was always nice enough to me, but I was never as close to her as I was to Uncle Lou. He was my blood relative, and I had no doubt she was a fine woman, born in Shrewsbury, supposedly introduced to Uncle Lou at a barn dance when they were both in their early twenties. Uncle Lou had a sister, Aunt Ethel, who met Rosie at the same dance. The three of them apparently got along fine. So when Ethel got so crazy that she should have been put in a hospital, Aunt Rosie said she'd look after her right there on the farm. Ethel lived to be fifty-five. By the time she died, she didn't recognize anybody, refused to comb her hair, and talked incessantly, not to

Uncle Lou or Aunt Rosie, but to the people of her imagination, the people who carried on long and apparently witty conversations with her, people she knew from childhood but who never were visible to anybody but Aunt Ethel. Of course, she never did anybody any harm, but she wasn't any help around the farm either, inside or out. She was too busy keeping up with her friends.

Aunt Rosie would ask me, "Do you think she's getting worse?"

"Hard to say. Seems about the same," I'd say. And I was being honest. Not until toward the end of her life, when she died of pneumonia, did she sink down into what you'd call dementia. Then it was hard to make her eat. She wouldn't get out of bed to go to the toilet. And over the course of a month or so, she stopped talking altogether, even to her invisible friends.

Aunt Rosie took the death in stride. "God bless her," she said with a deep sincerity that surprised me. "She hung in there all those years. It wasn't her fault."

The older I got and the more Aunt Rosie confided in me, the more I realized that a strain of insanity ran in my side of the family. Uncle Lou suffered from it too, but it wasn't as crippling for him as it was for his sister.

"Well, he's not exactly normal," Aunt Rosie said, sitting at the kitchen table one September morning while Uncle Lou and the men cut corn for the silo.

"Of course, I've noticed some things," I said.

"But it doesn't do any harm," she said. "He's a good man. Lots of people around here, from the old families, are a little crazy."

"Sort of like the Hatfields and McCoys down in Virginia?" I said.

"No, not dangerous. No feuds or anything like that. Mostly God-fearing people like your uncle. I guess marrying somebody like me from a little distance helps out. Nobody around here marries his first cousin. Did you ever meet the Comstock boy from town? A smart young man. He's marrying a girl from up in Burlington. No problem there. I suspect the craziness, or whatever it is, will all die out one of these days."

"Is Uncle Lou talking more than usual?" I asked. It was the first time I'd asked her directly about Uncle Lou's mental state.

"Just about the same, I'd say. He spends a lot of time on his music."

Only later did I know what she meant by "his music."

Only God knew what poor old Aunt Ethel had discussed with her multitude of friends. But it was different with her brother, Uncle Lou. His invisible friends must have been extremely witty, strong competitors for Jack Benny or Bob Hope. More than once, I'd seen Uncle Lou stop his tractor in the middle of the field because he was laughing too hard to see where he was going.

"You know," Aunt Rosie said, "it's like he slips into another world, like there was some sort of screen between us and . . . well, whatever it is, and he goes through it. He's not trying. It's where he finds himself. It's nowhere I can go."

I remembered a book I'd read many years ago. Written by a Princeton professor. He theorized that the Old Testament prophets actually heard "God's voice." They weren't kidding when they said God spoke to them. But their ability was bred out of us humans, like a bad trait is bred out of livestock. Now only the shamans in the deepest jungles hear those things, slip into another world with the help of drugs and dancing. I always thought that was a fascinating theory. Uncle Lou didn't do drugs or much dancing, but I doubt that Noah or Job did either.

Aunt Rosie said, "We can be sitting here having supper, and all of a sudden, he'll look up as if someone came into the kitchen. Then he'll sort of remember I'm there and come back. When he's with me, he doesn't talk to them . . . whoever they are. I think he's afraid I'll have him put away. But when he's alone, on the porch, say, when I'm cleaning up, I'll hear him chatting and laughing like he was with an old friend. When I get there, he shuts up and smiles at me as if nothing was going on. I'm used to it. It's no bother. But you asked."

"He doesn't drink much, does he?" I asked.

"Of course not. I wouldn't put up with that. Ethel did a bit of drinking when she was young. It didn't help her much, did it? Lou knows that liquor could be worse than poison for him."

When Uncle Lou was getting so arthritic it was hard for him to do the farming, and I had really gotten to know him and Aunt Rosie, he decided to buy a piano. And a couple months later, he called me in Boston and asked me to mail him some music paper. He couldn't find any in Bennington.

"You become a composer?" I asked, pretty mystified.

"You could call it that," he chuckled. "More a stenographer, I'd say."

The next time I visited, I asked Aunt Rosie if the music paper had arrived.

"Oh, yes. I think he's gone through most of it."

"What's it all about?"

"He tells me he hears music and writes it down. Simple as that. He says that's the way all music is written. That's the way Mozart and Beethoven did it. Would you say that's the truth?"

"I have no idea," I said. "I guess you could say they heard it before they wrote it down. Or played it first probably. Does he play too?"

"Just sort of with one finger," she said. "And he doesn't mind if I hear it. He won't talk in front of me, but he likes to fiddle with the piano. Doesn't bother me."

The two of them went to bed early, soon after dark, and I decided I was going to be a nosey parker. An old piano bench had come with the piano. When I lifted the seat, the compartment was full of music paper, the notes written tightly next to each other and, as far as I could see, only melody lines, no accompaniments. There must have been fifty sheets in fairly neat untied piles, just carefully stacked. I took a sheet from the middle of one of the stacks. Thievery, pure and simple, but I suspected Uncle Lou never looked back at music once it was written down. His handwriting, his notation, was amazingly crisp and professional looking. Where the hell had he learned that?

When I was saying good-bye at the end of that trip, Uncle Lou told me he was going to take a trip. He'd never even been to Boston as far as I knew.

"Where to?" I asked.

"Down to the Southwest, I think. Someplace sandy. Maybe Texas. They have deserts in Texas, don't they?"

"I guess," I said. "All over that part of the country."

"Palm trees? Date palms?"

"Gee," I said. "That's not my territory."

"They must have wells," he said. "They call them oases, don't they?"

"You're not going to find many oases in Dallas or Houston," I smiled. "Maybe way out in the country."

"Oh, they have oases, I promise you that."

"OK, if you say so."

"I may be on a trip the next time you come to visit," he said. "Your Aunt Rosie will look after you just fine."

"I'll check with her. Maybe I'll wait till you get back."

"Long wait," he said. "But whatever you want."

When I got home, I took the stolen sheet of music to my own piano. I saw that there were no bar lines, no meter or tempo specified, no whole notes or dotted notes, just plain black notes, one after another in tight succession, carefully placed on the music paper's printed lines.

I played the notes rather slowly and carefully, having no trouble reading his music. It had no perceptible rhythm, no beginning or end, just a continual flow of notes within a scrupulously observed range. It could have been easily sung by a tenor or baritone, even a bass with a little effort on the higher notes.

I turned the sheet over. The back was just as heavily inscribed as the front. I played it a bit more confidently. I had almost finished the second page when I suddenly had to stop. Something had dawned on me. I almost cried eureka! To say I couldn't believe my eyes would be putting it mildly.

Uncle Lou had written plainchant, the music of the earliest Christian monks, lines that were sung on one breath, then a pause, then another long, long line, unbroken by bar lines, unaccompanied for centuries, no part-singing, no harmonies, just one note after another and another and another.

Uncle Lou had been hearing plainchant. How it happened I'll never know. But then, how did Wagner bring back the ancient Nordic gods?

I waited a decent month or so. Then I called Aunt Rosie.

"You know you're always welcome," she said. "Uncle Lou isn't here right now, though."

"Where did he go?" I asked.

"He was talking about Texas, but I'm really not sure."

"Have you heard from him?" I asked. I tried to act only casually interested. I was actually feeling rather panicky.

"I haven't heard a word," she said. "But he was laughing a lot the day he left."

And neither of us ever heard another word, not a single word.

THE CURSE

"It's time we did something about that bastard," Clive said.

"I'm all for it," I said. "Know any assassins?"

We were riding downtown on the Chicago Rapid Transit bus.

"Murder is not the only option," Clive said.

"No, but it would be effective."

"I may have a better solution. Violence isn't always the weapon of choice."

Clive was my next-door neighbor. Born in England, Liverpool, and in his late thirties like me.

"So what are you suggesting?"

"Come over after dinner. Eight o'clockish. I may have an idea."

We parted on the sidewalk in front of my building. Clive worked two blocks away at Martin's Men's Clothing, very upscale, a perfect place for a naturalized Englishman with an Oxbridge accent.

I was a copywriter at Allyson Advertising, the second largest agency in Chicago. I loved the writing, hated my boss. Carl Jackson was his name. Group leader. Two or three famous campaigns to his credit. A bachelor, paunchy, fiftyish, pale as the underside of a fish, and not much loved by those of us in his group.

He'd come over to my desk, usually first thing in the morning, with a piece of copy I'd written.

"This needs work, Mr. Kirby" was his standard remark. Most people called me Stan.

"Any suggestions?" I'd learned to ask, knowing it would irritate him.

"That's your job," he'd say. "But I'll tell you this, kiddo, it just doesn't sing."

I'm glad to say my advertising instructor at Johnson Community never talked about "singing," and he'd also make specific suggestions. Jackson just kept asking for more, for different, for jazzy. I used to lie awake at nights trying to make an ad for sink detergent sing.

Or he'd move my desk. He did it twice.

Pointing to a deserted dusty desk in the corner, he'd say, "I want you over there. We have a girl, a management trainee, coming up for two weeks. I hear she's bright as hell."

"Figure she might be president someday? Time to suck up a little?"

"God, you've got a lip, kid. Someday it's going to get you in real trouble."

Under the circumstances, and under Carl Jackson, it's surprising any of my work ever saw the light of day. My wife, God bless her, always managed to notice my magazine ads. I figured if I could transfer out of Jackson's group and into one with better clients, I'd be writing TV in no time. (I might add that my wife—Helen, by name—who really loved her second-graders at Lincoln Elementary, managed to cheer her head off at every summer softball game of our interagency league. I'd been playing second base for the two years I'd been with Allyson.)

One day, Jackson came over to my desk, returning a piece of copy. "Your wife teaches second grade, right?"

"Yes, Lincoln." I couldn't imagine what was coming next. I knew it wasn't going to be pleasant since he'd never said anything pleasant to me in the past two years.

He dropped the piece of copy onto my desk. "I'd be very surprised if she couldn't write a better piece of prose than this."

"I wouldn't be surprised," I said. My insides began to tighten up.

"Maybe you should trade jobs."

I managed to say, "I'm sure she'd do a fine job."

A rare smile—no, a smirk—appeared on his face. "Ever think of another profession? You might be happier. You're looking sort of flushed this morning."

All I could do was nod. I didn't trust my voice. He nodded, gave me a sickening smile, and went back into his office.

**

I knew my English friend's store stayed open until seven to catch a customer or two after normal working hours. So his invitation for eight wouldn't leave him much time for supper.

"I haven't the foggiest idea what he **wants**," I said to Helen. "We were discussing the evil monster, Carl **Jackson, and** Clive said he had an idea."

"What about?" she said.

"Who knows? Perhaps he has an old **English** poison I could slip into the bastard's morning coffee."

"But poison wouldn't hurt him. It doesn't work on trolls. Your only hope is for him to be run over by a steamroller." She laughed. She knew how I felt about Jackson, but she didn't actually have a mean bone in her body. If a steamroller had really come into sight, she would have pulled Jackson—or Adolf Hitler—out of the way.

"The Brits used to send their convicts to Australia," I said. I was obviously clutching at straws. Hell, I was ready to clutch at anything. "Maybe Clive has a friend in Sydney who could offer a huge job to Jackson. An irresistible offer. God! Wouldn't that be a stroke of luck? He doesn't have a family to worry about. And Australia would be more humane than a steamroller."

"No family?" she said. "The women and children of Chicago are sure deprived!"

"Maybe I could get transferred to another group," I said. "I should really work at it. It couldn't possibly result in out of the frying pan, into the fire. Getting out of Jackson's frying pan could only result in ecstasy, unbounded joy, an occasional good night's sleep."

I waited until eight-thirty before going over to Clive's. His wife, Madeleine, a sweet lady from St. Louis, was washing up the dinner dishes. She and my wife were good friends. Helen usually went over to chat in the late afternoon before I got home.

"Well, hello," she greeted me. "What are you doing here? Nice to see you! Cup of coffee?"

"Thanks. Just had two cups. One more and I wouldn't get to sleep until Sunday. Clive thinks he has a way to make me happier at work. He's a kind man."

"I've noticed," she said. "How is he going to make you happier?"

"No idea."

"I didn't know you were so unhappy. Helen said you might move to another group. That's all."

"That would make me happy. It's just that my boss is a pig."

"Oh my! That bad, is it? Maybe Clive thinks you should be selling suits and shirts along with him. That way you'd get to meet a dozen or so pigs every day."

That remark surprised me. I'd never heard Clive complain about his job. We seldom discussed it. I didn't want Clive to think I was acting superior. Selling suits wasn't quite as snazzy as writing copy. Not quite as high up the social scale. Still, I figured he made as much as I did, maybe more.

Clive must have heard my voice. He came into the kitchen.

"Hi," he said, patting my shoulder. "I was afraid you'd forgotten." He had changed from his business suit into jeans and a baggy sweater. "Come on into the study." He kissed his wife on the cheek. "Man talk," he said. "Very private."

His study was the size of most small bedrooms in Chicago's developments. Nice windows, wall-to-wall carpeting, some old photos that were probably from his English childhood, a heavy old desk, and a couple of very comfortable easy chairs. I knew this was his private space. I imagined Madeleine was only allowed in to do an occasional dusting.

Clive said, "I just have three questions."

"Shoot."

"First, would you like a glass of port?"

I laughed. "Ah, a most serious question. Sure, I'd love one."

He pointed me to a chair by the window and turned to a cupboard that revealed several bottles of wine and hard liquor. He poured me a small glass and saluted me with one of his own. "Here's to the success of our mission."

His toast made me think of the eighteenth-century explorers who sailed out of England for the South Seas, for Australia, and were saluted by their king and cheered by their crews.

"Hear, hear," I said and sipped at my port. "So tell me more about the mission."

"Now," he said, "Would you mind if something unpleasant happened to your boss—Jackson, is it?—if nobody knew you were involved, and you got transferred to a job you liked better?"

"Now, hold on," I said. "Let's not get crazy. I don't want to get involved in the perfect crime, which always, always turns out to be rather imperfect."

"Crime?" said Clive. "Who said anything about crime? Our hands would be clean as an angel's wing. We would be way beyond the reach of the law. I promise you."

"There's no damned reason you should get involved in my office politics, just because I bitch to you on the bus—"

"Would you mind if I tried a little experiment?"

"I don't think we should be trying experiments. I'll be OK. Don't worry." I was suddenly wary of Clive's "experiment." God knows what he had up his sleeve. It sounded somehow dangerous.

Clive said, "You won't be involved, I promise." Obviously, I wasn't going to be able to divert him from his plan. Perhaps I should have just walked out. In retrospect, of course, I should have. But I must admit I was curious.

"Well," I said. "What's the third question? Or have you asked me three already?"

Clive stared at me for a second or two. "Can you get me a toad?"

"Yay-zoo," I said. "You want a toad? What the hell for?"

"Please, dear boy. Can you find one? Will you try?"

That's when it dawned on me. That's when I remembered a story Clive had told me a year earlier, soon after we moved in. It had shocked me then, and I still found it shocking. He had told me that his mother, back in Liverpool, belonged to a coven. A group of witches. She had risen to be leader of the group before she died. As a boy, he had loved to hear about her exploits. His father had thought she was loony, but the boy had believed her, admired her, and remembered her with great fondness. Soon after she died, Clive and his father had come to the United States. His father was still living in Boston.

It was impossible, frankly, for me to just say, "You're full of it." And now that I knew what he was up to, I was curious to see how it worked and, at the same time, absolutely positive it would work no wonders on my situation at the agency. Besides, Clive was a good friend, a next-door neighbor, and I knew he was dead serious about this witchcraft.

With a smile, rather like Doubting Thomas, I suppose, I said, "Sure. I'll look for a toad. I think I've seen some in the field out back."

"Oh, great," Clive said. He was beaming. "Great! And one other thing. I don't think it would be a good idea to tell Helen about this. I probably won't discuss it with Madeleine."

"You're going to do something witchy, aren't you?" I shook my head in disbelief. "You honestly think it can do some good."

"I know it can. Trust me. It can do a lot of good."

"Do you do a lot of this sort of thing?"

"Never. This is my first chance. But I heard a lot about it from my mother. I told you about it, didn't I? I haven't discussed it with anybody else. Of course, Madeleine knows, but we don't discuss it. It's safe to say she is not a believer."

"And you think I am?"

"I think you are not. I think you are merely humoring a friend, biting your tongue, trying not to be offensive to a next-door neighbor. You have a saintly patience. You are strong but gentle. That boss does not deserve you."

"That's me all right," I said. "OK." I emptied my glass and got up. "When will the wizard be needing his toad?"

"The sooner the better, don't you think? If you catch one, it'll live for ages in a glass jar. Mother always had one handy, and I don't remember her ever needing to go toad hunting. Just let me know when you have one, and we'll proceed. I'll proceed, that is. You won't have a thing to do."

"Like the joke says, 'He wanted a watch for Christmas, so they let him.'"

"Of course. It's up to you. We'll do a doubleheader. Teach Mr. Jackson a lesson he won't soon forget, and get you another job in the agency."

I must admit the prospects sounded good. But of course, they were crazy.

**

Saturday turned out to be a perfect day for toad hunting. I caught a fat beauty in fifteen minutes, dropped it into a jar, and put it onto the back porch.

"What in heaven's name is that for?" Helen asked a minute later when she spotted it. She'd been in the basement with the laundry while I was out on my brief hunting expedition.

"One of the Rosen boys asked if I'd catch him a toad for science class."

"Oh, come on. What is he, in third grade?"

"They learn fast these days."

"Of course they do. Mine certainly do. All geniuses. But the Rosen boys?"

I shrugged and proceeded to sweep the porch. The toad turned in the jar to keep his eye on the broom. I thought of feeding him, but I had no idea what he ate, and Clive had insisted toads didn't need any attention. Mine didn't look particularly unhappy.

Clive appeared on his back porch. He looked over, and I gave him a big thumbs-up. He did some silent clapping, pointed to his wristwatch, and held up five fingers. So I gave him another thumbs-up. If Helen had plans for the evening, they wouldn't start as early as five o'clock.

At five, I tucked the toad jar under my jacket and crossed to Clive's back porch. He was waiting for me.

He whispered, "She's taking a nap."

We walked as quietly as possible to his study. The curtains were pulled. He turned on a dim light in the bookcase.

"You do have it?" he asked.

I pulled the jar from under my coat.

He took the jar and studied the toad. "Oh, a beauty. Perfect. Well done. Sit down if you want to stay."

As I sat down, he pulled a good-sized metal pot from a cupboard under the window. Also a tray laden with small porcelain containers, the size of cigarette packs. Dipping into those little jars, he dropped things into the pot, things that looked like cloves, like flower petals, like salt or sand, like pieces of tree bark, and some clear liquids and some thick syrups like molasses. I'd be hard put to describe the smell. All the while, he kept up a sort of mumbling conversation with himself, his left hand stirring with a carved wooden spoon, his right hand dropping in the ingredients.

He turned to me. "Your boss is left-handed or right-handed?"

"Left-handed."

"Good. It's easier that way."

He picked up the glass jar, reached in for the toad, and held it over the potion pot. It wiggled a bit. Then he tore off one of its back legs. I was horrified at the cruelty. I may have gasped, but I gritted my teeth. He dropped the leg into the pot and put the maimed toad back in its jar. Then he turned to me.

"There. We're done. Sorry about the toad, but it was absolutely necessary. These traditions, these recipes, have to be followed exactly."

I stood up to leave. "Good luck," I said. "Let me know if it works."

"No, no. You must let *me* know if it works. You'll know Monday morning."

"You're sure?" I laughed. "You didn't forget any ingredients?"

"Keep your fingers crossed."

'OK. See you on the bus on Monday. And thanks for making the effort."

**

We didn't have much to say Monday morning. I'm sure we were both thinking of the same thing. Would anything, anything at all, be different at the agency?

I had barely sat down at my desk when I saw Jackson get off the elevator and go into his office. He didn't acknowledge me or anyone else. I started to sift through the assignments on my desk.

But just fifteen minutes later, he came over to my desk.

"Morning," he said. "How are you? Good weekend?" Unusually friendly for Jackson.

"Just fine, thanks. You too?"

"I have good news this morning, good for both of us. Bill Tennyson has asked if I could spare you for a while on his sweetener account. And I said yes. Hope you don't mind."

"No problem," I said. "He's a nice guy." I instantly thought of Clive's shenanigans.

"It'll be a nice change for you."

I heard myself saying, "And for you, right?"

"I suppose," he muttered. "Feel free to move down there any time."

As he walked away, I carefully studied the way he walked, the way he swung his arms, the way he carried his head. He looked exactly the way he had before Clive's witchcraft efforts. I was not surprised, but I thought Clive would be disappointed more than a little.

As for myself, I was in seventh heaven. *Jubilant* isn't too strong a word. At least my part of the potion had worked. Bill Tennyson was the best-liked senior writer in the agency. If I'd been asked to choose a boss, I would have named Bill. I almost called Helen with the good news, but then I decided not to pull her out of class. And Clive had made it clear he didn't appreciate private calls at work.

So I joined the Tennyson group, piling up on my desk all the background research on that famous sweetener, all the focus group results, even the list of chemicals that went into it. I knew from my experience with Jackson that it would take a day or two, perhaps a week, to get on track with all the musts and no-nos of a new account.

As I left the office, a little later than usual, admittedly to make a good first impression, I decided to buy Helen a bunch of celebratory flowers. Roses. A dozen bright red roses. I might even insist we go out for dinner. I knew she'd want to share in my good luck.

Good luck? Or maybe something else? I couldn't wait to tell Clive.

When I got home, I found Helen sitting in the kitchen, a cup of coffee beside her, her face red with crying, too upset even to get up.

"What in God's name's the matter?" I said. "Tell me." I stood still, tense with apprehension.

She clenched her fists in her lap. "Clive's dead," she managed to say. "He came home an hour ago and . . . and died. I was there."

"My God! What was it? Heart?"

"Madeleine doesn't know. All she said was, 'He made a mistake.' And then she couldn't say anything else. I don't think he'd been sick. His jacket was all torn. She helped him out of it. And then he just crumbled. I came back from over there a minute ago. I told her I'd make her something for supper. It's terrible. You shouldn't see him. Nobody should."

"Why shouldn't I?"

"His arm. It's all black and blue, withered up, and covered with blood. The sleeve of his shirt is torn to rags. It looks like something clawed at it. Please don't go see it."

I noticed the roses in my hand. "I'll take these over," I said. "They were for you. But I'll take them over to Madeleine."

"Don't try to see him. Please."

"I won't. I just can't imagine . . ."

And so ended Clive's efforts at witchcraft, poor guy. Maybe he forgot an ingredient. Or maybe it was really bad luck. And the whole point was just to get a better job for me.

I guess he was showing off a little, too. And maybe I should have stopped him right at the beginning. Or laughed at him. Or told his wife what he was doing.

But how come his wife said, "He made a mistake?" She must have already known what he was doing. Did he confide in her that he made a mistake? Should he have used one of the toad's front legs instead of a rear? Or was some of his mumbling wrong?

These are questions I'm sure I'll take with me to my grave.

As for Clive, I'm afraid he was just another poor guy who made a terrible mistake.

THE YOUNG PIGS

He trotted toward the barn. He imagined the Johnson twins would get there ahead of him. They were prompt for everything. If he was late, he could blame it on Mr. Conklin. Maybe the old Vermonter was reluctant to give his approval because he didn't want twelve-year-old boys like Jackie and the twins to be in on the killing. He warned it wouldn't be fun. Jackie didn't care. He knew he and his buddies were going to find it darned exciting.

The Johnson boys were already in the gloomy horse barn. Still called the horse barn, but no horses anymore, not since tractors and cars. The boys were standing perfectly still, watching. Glen Westcott and his helper stood in front of the middle box stall. Its door was open. A trough had been placed across the opening, not a good fit, leaving a couple of feet at each end. But the two young pigs didn't mind. They were snuffling around in the trough, eating, glancing up, and chewing some more. Many months older than piglets, about halfway to full grown.

Glen Westcott ran the farm for Mr. Conklin. Jackie thought he was pretty grim, always civil when Jackie was exploring the farmyard but never what you'd call friendly. Had other things on his mind. Jackie wondered if he ever changed his clothes, even for church. Heavy jeans, dark work shirt, muddy boots. Pretty much the same for his helper, whose name Jackie could never remember.

Glen Westcott told the boys to stand back. They retreated a couple of feet to the opposite stalls. The aisle was narrow. They still had a good view of the trough and the pigs. The sun shone through a high window onto the golden straw lying heavy in the pigs' stall. Glen wanted to make the pigs comfortable, Jackie thought.

Glen had a rifle hanging on his arm. He looked at his helper and raised his eyebrows. The helper nodded. Glen lowered his rifle to within two inches of the first pig's head and shot it right between the eyes. The blast was deafening.

One of the Johnson twins covered his ears. Both pigs jumped back. Glen shot the second one in the side of the head, right above its ear. Jackie could see the black hole where the bullet went in.

And then the screaming began. Jackie had never heard anything like it. Not even vaguely like it. Maybe a little like human screams you heard in movies. Screeching, ear-splitting evidence of excruciating pain.

The pigs ran frantically around the stall, bumping into the walls, stumbling in the straw. Not looking for a way out, just fleeing, screaming, and fleeing.

Glen stepped into the stall, caught hold of one pig's ear, pulled its head up, and cut its throat. He stabbed it and then sliced an inch or two in each direction. He stepped back as the pig tried to continue its run. The blood gushed from its neck. Halfway around the stall, its front legs gave way, and it collapsed.

As Glen was killing the first pig, his helper killed the second. No more screaming. A little twitching in the straw. Eyes not moving. Gushing blood slowing down.

The rifle blasts rang in Jackie's ears. But far louder, far more horrifying, was the screaming, the endless, awful screaming. He had expected an exciting experience. But this . . . this . . . Then he thought he heard one of the Johnsons snicker. Or was he trying not to cry?

Jackie walked out into the sun, to the edge of the road, and vomited in the grass.

WHISTLE-BLOWER

Pete had never seen anything like it. Yes, he was young, only thirty-one, and had been in Geneva for only six months. But in New York, he'd been working with Plymouth, Inc., for six years, starting in the mailroom and rising to human resources manager of Plymouth's largest subsidiary, which by itself was the third largest advertising agency in the world. With the other subsidiaries, Plymouth was indisputably the largest worldwide advertising conglomerate.

Up until now, it had never crossed his mind that the international branch of Plymouth, headquartered here in Geneva, was anything but 100 percent ethical. That is, honest within the company and with the public and, of course, with its clients. In his years in New York, he had never noticed the slightest odor of dishonesty. He had jumped at the chance to spend two or three years in Europe Today, he found some things were different overseas.

He was walking up the hill toward the railroad station before turning north on Rue de Lausanne. The lake was behind him, trees on either side with their brightest spring flowers, the sun still warm at five in the afternoon. A few pedestrians but nothing like New York at rush hour. Geneva was businesslike but also relaxed and confident.

He shared an apartment with a young Brit who worked for the UN. Geneva's UN offices were only a bit smaller than the offices in New York, and many meetings that were not vital to U.S. interests took place in Geneva.

Gerard, Pete's apartmentmate, was with the disarmament office. "I expect it to be a lifetime assignment. Everybody talks the righteous line. But disarmament is as popular as midlife circumcision. Now, that makes you cringe, no? That's most people's reaction to disarmament if they're anywhere above the rank of church janitor."

He reached the apartment house the same time Pete did. They rode up in the elevator together. Both in suits and ties, well-tailored young six-footers, glad it was a Friday in May.

Pete said, "Where to this weekend?"

"London," said Gerard. "It's not that I'm homesick. It's just that I really can't remember what Lois looks like. Appalling! You know how loyal I am. Write to her once a week and she writes to me every Sunday. I can't even remember if she's blond or brunette. Do you remember? Perhaps warding off Russians and Japs all day has damaged my brain. Noticed anything, have you?"

"I thought that picture in your bedroom was Lois."

"Oh no. That's Isabelle. Swears she's the daughter of a baron, which I doubt, but unforgettable in bed. I hope you're well set up for the weekend."

"I was going to do Zurich. Haven't been there yet. But there's still snow down in Megeve. Won't be there forever." His life on the New England ski slopes had been interrupted by a nasty compound fracture of his right leg. It hadn't healed properly. He limped and expected to limp the rest of his life. But he was skiing again.

They shared a two-bedroom apartment in a five-year old building, arranged through the UN and Geneva's Chamber of Commerce, which Plymouth helped support. Men and women came and went in Geneva like in few other places in the world. The young men's apartment was on the fourth floor, with a good-sized living room, decently furnished, and with a great view of the lake. The kitchen was adequate for two noncookers. They spent most of their eating time in the restaurant conveniently located on the ground floor of the building.

When Pete had changed into jeans and a sweater, Gerard was already at the built-in bar mixing himself a martini. Then he sat down in the chair that had turned out to be his favorite. Pete was more than happy with the couch.

Pouring himself a good-sized vodka, Pete asked, "When's your London flight?"

"Seven-thirty. SAS. It comes from Cairo, I think. Should be full of screaming children suffering from uncontrollable diarrhea. Probably a goat or two. Always a treat."

"Maybe in a couple of weeks I'll be able to put the top down on the old Mustang."

Gerard said, "I read there are more chauffeur-driven sedans in Geneva than anywhere else in the world. When your vice president was here last week—not your favorite politician, I get the feeling—I counted six Cadillacs in his entourage alone."

Pete wasn't leaving for Megeve until the next morning. The two friends decided to have dinner together downstairs at Le Merlot Rouge.

"Redundant, don't you think?" Gerard had said.

"I'm not sure. Is there a white merlot?"

"Never heard of it."

"What the hell. The food's good."

They both ordered the steak frites with a salad and beer.

Gerard said, "I gather you had a ghastly day at your old puffery plant. Or are you merely reflecting my own jaundiced reaction to the new Hungarian foreign minister? He asked me if I was Australian. My God, what an ignoramus. Smelled funny, too."

"It was not my best day," Pete said.

"Screwed up, did you?"

"I did not screw up, for a change. But thanks for asking. No, something happened that shocked the hell out of me. Like finding out your mother had been married before meeting your father."

"To shock an old legionnaire like you, it must have been bloodcurdling."

"Just short of that. But let's talk about your Isabelle. Sounds great. Or is this weekend devoted to Lois? Dare I imagine a third lovely has entered the picture?"

After dinner, back upstairs, Gerard quickly packed his overnighter. "Now, don't break the other leg if you can help it," he said, heading for the door.

Pete said, "And don't you catch the clap again."

"Again? Never! I'm English, you know." And the door closed behind him.

Pete went to the window and looked at the lights reflected in the lake's water. He thought of what had happened that morning. He had responded at the time with total silence. Perhaps that was the wrong response. Perhaps he should tell somebody. At least discuss it. But with whom? Maybe when Gerard got back.

**

All the big brass from New York was in town. Seven men and one woman, led by the founder and chairman, Donald D. Fouts. These people were in Geneva to review the last year's results of the several subsidiaries functioning in Europe. The treasurer, a fat red-faced man wearing a green silk vest, had arrived from New York a day earlier to make sure the reports were clear and straightforward enough for nonaccountants. Simple charts were being created. Results were all that mattered. The big shots had more to do than review the nickel-and-dime operations of Frankfurt or Naples.

Pete's office was just across the hall from the conference room where the charts would be shown. The big table had been pulled back, making room for a dozen chairs facing an easel. The meeting was called for nine o'clock.

The charts arrived that morning in Pete's office as fast as the art department could finish them off. Simple bar charts, vertical, showing the past year's results contrasted with the former year's. Red for the past year and blue for two years ago.

The New York treasurer and the local art director stood beside Pete's desk, making a last minute check of the charts. Pete stood silently by, fascinated by the way a year's work by three thousand people could be reduced to a handful of red and blue bars.

The chart for Spain appeared. Pete watched the two men study it.

The treasurer said, "Uh-uh. Not on your life. Absolutely not."

Pete stretched to see. Two years ago was a better year than the recent year.

The treasurer said, "Get a magic marker and more of that red paint. Now!" He glanced up at Pete as the art director hurried out of the office. "It's no good showing Mr. Fouts the bad times in Madrid. Their records are all fucked up, always. He's due in Paris this afternoon. Big presentation. More important than the cha-cha castanet account or whatever the hell they have down there."

Pete knew the art department had worked directly from the reports sent in from the various cities. Their charts were accurate down to a quarter inch. They all showed decent gains except for Madrid. He'd heard rumors that that office was not too healthy, but its owner, Mr. Cabral, was an old golfing friend of Mr. Fouts, so the office remained immune to any efforts by Geneva to clean it up.

Plymouth, Inc., was a publicly traded company, listed on the New York and London stock exchanges, required to publish an annual report, expected to maintain its small dividend, competing against European and American companies that had been around fifty years longer than Plymouth.

Was it possible to alter the financial facts just to keep Mr. Fouts from missing his flight to Paris? Would this . . . well, fraud ever be corrected?

Plymouth had shareholders who could get nasty. What about the SEC? Would Mr. Cabral down in Madrid be quietly smirking and going to another bullfight?

The treasurer took the black magic marker from the art director and raised the top of the Madrid year's chart about two inches. A million dollars, Pete figured. He filled in the addition with the red marker. He stood back and looked at his handiwork.

"That's better. Will it dry?"

"It's dry already," the art director said. "Nice going!" He patted the treasurer's shoulder.

Pete had never known any whistle-blowers or thought much about them. But what courage it must take! Of course, you got fired, with a loss of salary and benefits. No company would hire you except maybe the Salvation Army. You'd be so hated at your old company that nobody would think twice about making up lurid lies about your behavior. Don't expect a good reference. Drunk? Queer? Schizo? And if you had a family, how delighted would they be to see your picture in the paper with a caption that suggested you were a traitor to your company and friends?

Pete wondered if he should try to talk to the vice-chairman, one of the men over from New York, the man who had hired him several years ago. But what would he say? He'd sound naive, unsophisticated. Perhaps a bad choice for this Geneva job. Like a little boy tattling on a playmate.

But when the presentation was over, the executives came out of the conference in a fast, tight bunch, like pro footballers making a big entry into the stadium. No chance for Pete to latch onto the vice-chairman. And anyway, he might just be laughed at. Or fired on the spot. Plymouth, Inc., had to be protected from crazies like Pete.

Maybe the thing to do was try to find another job. In Geneva? New York? And then after he'd settled in, then he could tell what he'd seen. Tell whom? By then, would it matter? Anyway, who would hire a man with a gimpy leg?

**

When Gerard got back Sunday night, he found Pete on the couch, watching TV.

"How was the skiing?"

"Darned good," Pete said. "And I took your advice. I didn't break my other leg."

"Oh, good thinking," Gerard said. "And Isabelle sends her love."

"Was she as fantastic as ever?"

"By the grace of God, Lois had to go with her mother to visit an aunt or somebody in Edinbrough. So Isabelle could be entertained without the slightest pang of conscience. And I'm beginning to think she really may be a baron's daughter. Rather impressive pictures around her flat. If she and I teamed up, what would that make me? An honorable, maybe? Or just a poor sod who seduced a baron's daughter."

"The marriage would take place at St. Paul's, right?"

"I should say so. I wouldn't stand for some shoddy little chapel down in Kent or someplace. I wonder where she comes from. I'll have to ask."

"Of course you'll want me as best man."

"An American? Well, I'd have to check with the archbishop. Quite unusual. But enough about me. Have you come to grips with that nasty problem you encountered at your office of disinformation? I forget what it was exactly."

Pete said, "Oh that. Nothing much. I thought it through, an American exercise you wouldn't understand, and decided there wasn't any real problem for me. Nothing I couldn't live with. And the skiing was wonderful. Sort of settled me down. You should try skiing someday. Good for the nerves."

"I find horizontal exercise far more beneficial. Exhausting, of course, but pleasant. Nevertheless, I'm a growing boy and need my sleep. Will you excuse me? It's almost midnight. My lonely mattress calls."

"Good night," Pete said. "I'll turn off the TV in a minute. Just have to see who the murderer was. We Americans are hounds for justice, you know."

"Oh, sure you are," Gerard said. "But I'm too tired to argue tonight. See you in the morning."

As Pete watched the end of the TV show, he realized he'd given up the whistle-blower idea. The skiing was just too good.

A VERMONTER IN PARIS

"Now, let's not have any death in Paris."

"What do you mean, death in Paris?"

"Just kidding." His daughter gave him a peck on the cheek. "You know, *Death in Venice*, the story of the old guy getting infatuated with the kid on the beach. Thomas Mann, I think."

"Seventy is not that old, thank you very much. And I haven't been infatuated with any boy since I was six years old and thought my brother John should have been Hollywood's next Tarzan."

"Wow. What a confession." She shook her head in mock amazement. "OK, dear Daddy. Just enjoy Paris." She took his arm as they headed for the departure lounge at the terminal. "Peter wanted to come see you off, but some sort of emergency came up."

"Every damned day's an emergency for a surgeon. He should have been a laid-back banker like me. Don't know what got into him."

"He sends love, and of course, he's paying for half."

He pressed her arm to his side. "And you the other half. Your mother was generous too. You must have inherited it from her, bless her. Don't think I don't appreciate it. I could've paid my own way."

"But it's your seventieth. Celebration time. Paris time. Bon voyage time. Have a ball."

"Come on. Give your elderly father a daughterly hug. I still love getting hugged."

She put her arms around his waist and her face next to his. "Au revoir," she whispered.

His plane took off a half hour later. She decided not to hang around.

**

He was still jet-lagged, which made him feel like an exhausted eighty, but he wanted to use every minute on this first visit to Paris. Nothing could improve on the month of May in Paris, probably the best weather in the world, with Renoir blue skies and Monet green grass, and girls in gauzy blouses.

His little hotel on the Rue de Lille was adequate—his room with its own bathroom en suite, which was elegant and rare on the Left Bank in that year of 1952, perhaps a bit decadent. He would remember to thank his daughter's travel agent. The lady manager, or concierge, or receptionist, or whatever her title, was named Madame Claire. Cooly proper, not unfriendly, big chested and crimson lipped, reading the daily paper in the small room off the lobby. Black clothes, along with high heels, apparently made up the uniform of Parisian women over forty, at least the ones he had seen. He had expected French women to be a little more colorful.

His name was Mel, short for Melville, Mel Swanson. Six feet tall, beginning to stoop, still in good shape, gray hair cut short, and, that first morning, wearing a light gray suit with a bright red tie from Maxons on Main Street in Burlington. Jet lag made his heavy leather shoes feel even heavier.

In careful English, he asked Madame Claire, "Where is a sidewalk cafe where I can get breakfast?"

"Right up the Rue d'Abbe," she said, pointing up the street. "Two blocks to Montmartre. The Cafe Flore. They have eggs and bacon until noon. Maybe later. Everybody here sleeps late."

He thanked her and stepped onto the sidewalk. Perhaps he should have worn his golf jacket instead of the suit coat. The few others, perhaps students, on the narrow cobbled street were in jeans and sockless sandals. He felt overdressed and rather old, like the warden at a juvenile center. But why waste time going back to change. Madame Claire should have warned him.

The Cafe Flore and its broad tree-lined avenue were bustling with men, women, children, unleashed dogs, policemen, priests, and dozens of sparrows foraging among the cafe's tables, the bravest ones actually on the tables. Mel felt he was the only man in Montmartre wearing a suit that hot spring Saturday, perhaps the only suit-wearer in Paris.

He spotted an empty table and managed to get to it just ahead of a brown-skinned girl with her hair all beaded and braided, wearing an orange ankle-length dress that started just above her breasts. Mel hadn't noticed her until he had plunked down in a straw-seated chair and found her standing next to him, staring and frowning, muttering something that didn't sound complimentary, and finally walking back to the sidewalk. When he looked up, his neighbors quickly looked away. He was not only a tourist in a red tie and heavy brown shoes, but he was also typically uncivilized, refusing to share his table with a lovely Nigerian princess.

His table was up against the side of the building, right outside an open window. The cooking smells were nice. He watched the traffic jam on the boulevard, the human traffic jam on the sidewalk with most people on the alert for an empty table, some people walking up to the corner and back, over and over, waiting for their table luck to change.

An elderly white-aproned waiter finally arrived at Mel's table. Mel carefully said, "Bacon and eggs please." He looked hopefully at the waiter, who continued to stare at him as if he hadn't heard. Mel repeated, "Bacon and eggs, please."

"I hear," said the waiter. And proceeded, frowning, to babble a blue streak. In French. The neighbors who had disapproved of Mel's snubbing of the African girl frowned at him again. He stared at the scarred tabletop in front of him while the waiter ranted on and on. He looked up when the waiter ran out of breath. Standing beside the table was a young man smiling at him, Mel's first smile in Paris.

"May I translate?" the young man asked.

Mel felt a burden of apprehension lifted from his shoulders. "Please do. Just in time."

"Would you mind if I joined you?"

"Not at all." Mel gestured to a chair. "Be my guest. I thought I spoke a little French, but . . ."

"Don't worry. Nobody can understand what dear Josef says." He looked up at the waiter and winked. "Right, Josef?"

Josef said, "And?"

The young man said, "Just coffee. Black. Like your heart."

Josef said, "Eggs, bacon, and coffee." He jotted down something in code, slipped it under the sugar bowl, and left.

Mel extended his hand. "My name is Mel Swanson. You arrived in the nick of time. I might have fled back to the States."

They shook hands. "My name's Ron, sir," the young man said.

"Just call me Mel. And please, no *sir*. Just Mel. Are you American too?"

"Mother is. My father's Danish. Mother always speaks English to me. Is it pretty good?"

"It's perfect," Mel said. "I guess you look more like your father. All that blond hair. It looks good parted in the middle. I combed mine that way when I was your age, back when I still had some hair to comb. Nobody does that in the States. Not at the moment, at least." Why was he rambling and reminiscing with this kid, this stranger? He was silent while Josef delivered their coffee.

"If you're from Denmark, I suppose you're a skater."

"Oh yes, indeed. I'm a goalie. Just squat in front of the net and get shot at. Is *squat* the right word?"

"Good as any, I guess. I'm from a northern state, Vermont. Lots of skating there too." He wondered when he last put on skates. Fifty years ago? Jesus! He sipped at his coffee.

"I never heard of Vermont. But I will. I'm doing American Social Studies at university. I finish my first year in a couple of weeks. It'll be my twenty-first birthday, too. Is Vermont near Texas?"

"Not quite. But on the same continent. So happy birthday in advance." His eggs and bacon arrived. "You must be here on some sort of education visa. Right?"

"It ran out six weeks ago." He lowered his voice to a hoarse whisper. "I'm illegal. They may throw me into the Bastille. People rot in the Bastille, don't they? Is *rot* the right word?"

"They certainly do. They say it's very damp. I'd choose Copenhagen any day."

"I'll go home after school. I'm sort of homesick. When are you going home?"

"In two weeks. My kids gave me this trip for my seventieth birthday."

"Wow. You're seventy? Nice going. But you don't know Paris?"

"God no. This is my first morning."

"Want a guide?"

"You?"

"Me." He pointed playfully at his chest. "I'm real cheap, but a man's got to live."

"Let me buy you dinner."

"I'm busy at dinner. But I'll meet you at eleven. How about right here? A bit of Paris after dark."

"Right there on the sidewalk?"

"Sure."

"I may be walking in my sleep, but I'll be here."

The young man drank the last drops of his coffee. "You've got a date with the best guide in Paris." He offered his hand, and Mel shook it.

As the young man picked his way through the tables, Mel realized what an athlete he was. Tall, broad shouldered, graceful. And he spoke English.

**

The Louvre filled two of his afternoon hours. The gallery jammed with Greek and Roman statuary amazed him. He could not see any difference between Greek athletes and Roman generals, and he wondered if any students at the University of Vermont could make the distinction. The Romans, at least, wore togas. The Greeks decidedly did not.

He spent only half an hour with the impressionists. How many galleries did they inhabit? After fighting the crowd in the first two, he headed for the fresh air. He could feel the sweat in his armpits and on his chest. The Louvre's air-conditioning could not handle the summer crowds. He would come back the next day. Maybe Sunday would be quieter.

A small restaurant on the Rue Jacob near his hotel provided an English-speaking waiter and some good roast chicken. He picked a wine at random from the list. It was good. He had a second glass. The melon was wonderfully sweet.

Back at the hotel, he napped until his alarm clock went off. He might have shaved but merely slathered on some aftershave lotion. He wore the golf jacket and decided he looked sporty in the red tie. He arrived at the Cafe Flore with fifteen minutes to spare. He felt like a sore thumb standing on the sidewalk, being jostled by Saturday nighters with a few glasses of wine already under their belts. Mel kept checking his pocket for his wallet. And glancing at his watch. And looking up and down the sidewalk.

Then he heard a shout. "Hey, Mel! Right here!"

He looked to his left, then his right.

"Here, Mel!"

Right there in front of him, up against the curb, and holding up traffic, was Ron in a crimson convertible. A small one, with matching crimson seats. Mel could not have been more surprised if Ron had arrived on horseback.

"Come on. Get in," Ron yelled over the bedlam of honking horns.

Mel could not find a handle. So he stepped right over the door and dropped into the seat. He knew that half of Paris was staring at him. And at the red convertible. And at the blond athlete.

"How do you like it?" Ron laughed and patted Mel's shoulder in greeting.

"Fantastic. What a surprise. Yours?"

"Yes indeed. But don't ask where I got it. Or how."

Suddenly they swerved into a narrow side street without slowing down.

"You're going to love it. The Fiacre. Can't tell the boys from the girls. But it doesn't matter, does it?"

Mel had only a vague idea of what Ron was shouting at him. "No. Not at all. Great idea."

The little square where they parked was only a quarter mile from the Cafe Flore, but it was as silent as if it were in a far country. A single streetlight. A distinguished marble bust on a pedestal. Probably not the founder of this bar of Ron's.

Ron grabbed Mel's arm and pulled him along. A simple sign hung over the door. Ron went in first. The noise of music and shouting was almost as surprising as the outdoor silence. The walls must have been padded to totally contain that level of noise. Or maybe cigarette smoke was a noise inhibiter.

The room was only a little bigger than Mel's two-car garage back in Burlington. At one end was the door they had just entered, a couple of feet from the bottom of steep stairs leading straight up to the next floor. At the other end was a tiny stage, shared by an upright piano and a bar. The pianist was a middle-aged man wearing a clown's whiteface and a red rubber-ball nose. The bartender was a lithe young African wearing a tasseled Turkish fez and a silver jock strap. In the area between the door and the stage were fifty men and four women, give or take a handful of each.

Right across from the front door was a banquette and narrow table. Ron pushed Mel toward it. Its two occupants nodded and smiled and left to join the milling crowd in the middle

"How you doing?" Ron shouted. "You OK?"

"Fine," said Mel. "Love that horse." He pointed to the horse's head mounted over the door. Somebody had cut ear holes in an old straw hat and jammed it onto the horse. "Maybe this is where the expression, 'how's your old straw hat?' originated."

"Never heard that one. Can I get you a drink? What do you want?"

"Scotch and water," Mel said. He reached for his wallet.

"No, it's on me," said Ron, shaking a finger at Mel. "It'll take a minute. You sure you're all right?"

"I'll be better with a drink."

"Coming up. And do me a favor. Take off that tie."

Mel obliged, tucking the tie into his back pocket. He looked more closely at the crowd. Mostly men in their late teens or twenties. One white-haired man was evoking hysterical laughter from his surrounding young listeners.

Apparently, a wit of Wildean dimensions. Silent young men holding beer bottles leaned against the walls, eyes alert, aware of the hilarity in the middle of the room and of each other.

Mel felt alone, foreign, and old. Thank God this Ron was looking after him. Did the police raid places like this? They would in Vermont. New England frowned on having such a wonderful time. Fraternity boys were allowed to have fun, but others were guilty of disturbing the peace. Homosexuals were traditional disturbers of the peace. They committed other crimes, whatever they were. Sometimes they landed in jail.

As Ron returned with a beer and a scotch, a piano fanfare blared out, the pianist mimicking a trumpet. The lights dimmed, and a spotlight on top of the piano turned on and focused on the stairs, right above where Mel and Ron were sitting. Mel could make out people shouting "Hooray Pierre!"

Ron spoke into Mel's ear. "Pierre is coming down. He's the owner. Lives upstairs with his wife and four children. Rich as Croesus. A real nice guy."

Pierre was wearing a black suit, white shirt, a dark tie, and a thin mustache on a powdered face. One hand held on to the banister. In the other hand was a six-foot-long white scarf that he whirled around over his head like a cowboy with a lasso. At the bottom of the stairs, he came straight to Mel's narrow table, leaned over, and kissed Ron on the forehead.

"Ah bon soir," gurgled Pierre. His eyes flickered over Mel. Then in perfect English, "A new friend?"

"Yes," said Ron.

Pierre swished his scarf across both of their heads. "Love is grand, isn't it? Be good to each other." And he moved out to the crowd, which opened a path, and then closed behind him. His scarf kept appearing like whiffs of smoke puffing into the air.

They stayed another half hour. Ron brought another round of drinks. Young men came to their table and spoke to Ron. One said to Mel, "Hi, Daddy. You got a big star tonight." As each one left, Ron explained who they were. A painter, a medical student, a policeman, and a male whore who claimed he had been to bed with Rudolph Nureyev.

Once Pierre, the owner, climbed back up his stairs to his wife and four children, the bar quieted down. Pairs began to leave. The predators along the walls moved into the center like barracudas into a school of herring. The pianist played "Smoke Gets in Your Eyes" and "Just One of Those Things." Mel felt overwhelmingly tired. Ron put an arm across Mel's shoulders as they headed for the little red car.

"Want to go for a ride tomorrow?' he asked quietly in the silent street.

"Sure," said Mel. "Sounds nice."

"Versailles?"

"Wow! Sure. I'd love it."

"Lots of walking. Don't wear those wooden shoes or you'll be crippled."

"I'll get sneakers." He pulled out his wallet. "What do I owe you?"

"Oh come on. Why don't you buy me dinner tomorrow? Fair enough?"

"You're being damned generous. Damned kind. I appreciate it. We'll have a nice dinner."

At the Hotel de Lille, Ron reached across Mel's lap to open the door. Instinctively, Mel roughly pushed his arm away.

"Sorry," said Ron. "Just opening the door for you."

"I know," said Mel. "I'm so tired I don't know what I'm doing."

"Say good night to Madame Claire."

"You know her?"

"Everybody knows her. She was around even during the war. Tell her Ron says go to hell.'"

"Well, I think I'd be wiser not to. What time tomorrow?"

"It's Sunday, isn't it? I'm busy till two. Pick you up at three? Can you amuse yourself till then?"

"I'll try."

"Play chess with Madame Claire. They say she once beat Admiral Doenitz during the occupation."

"Great suggestion. See you tomorrow."

Madame Claire's thousand-year-old assistant smiled gruesomely as he crossed the lobby.

**

Madame Claire told him where he could find a men's clothing store that would be open on Sunday. She showed him a map and carefully pronounced the store's name in case he took a taxi.

He picked out a pair of white slacks with a navy blue stripe running down the sides. And a short-sleeved red sport shirt that he could wear for golf back home. And sneakers. The clerk talked him into a Greek sailor's cap with the traditional short visor. He figured he looked pretty good for a seventy-year-old on his way to Versailles.

When he came down from his room just before his three o'clock date, Madame Claire gave her approval. "Very stylish, monsieur. You are going to the country?"

"A friend is taking me to Versailles," he explained.

"Very good. You will have a nice time." She strolled with him to the front door.

When Ron arrived, as usual exactly on time, Mel waved a greeting and stepped onto the sidewalk.

"No, no," Madame Claire shouted. "Not that one! That is not your friend!"

Mel stopped in his tracks. Madame Claire grabbed his arm. "He will cut your throat and drink your blood!" She pointed an accusing finger at Ron and shouted something in French.

Ron yelled right back. In English he cried, "Bitch collaborator!"

Mel pushed Madame Claire's hand off his arm. "I'll be all right. But thanks for the warning. It'll all be just fine," he said. "He's my friend."

"You are a fool," she said. "He is not your friend!"

"Nothing to worry about," he said and got into the car.

"You are a fool!" She marched back into the hotel.

The car roared off at its usual high speed. Ron said, "She hates me, God knows why. Whenever she sees me, she raises hell. I've had friends in that hotel, and she's always telling them bad things about me."

"Maybe she's crazy," Mel said. "Or maybe she thinks you're somebody else."

"Well, she can think whatever she wants." Then he seemed to relax. They drove in silence for a minute. Ron said, "I've got to go home before we go to Versailles. Got to change my clothes. It'll just take a minute."

Mel noticed that he was wearing a very skimpy tee shirt that left him practically naked above the waist. And his shorts were so tight they must have made a mark on his thighs.

Ron said, "My friend likes to imagine we're on the beach at Cannes having a Sunday picnic. It's OK, but I feel like one of those 'living statue' guys at the Follies Bergeres." He glanced at Mel. "You look very nice."

They pulled up in front of an old apartment house. Mel had no idea where they were.

Ron said, "Do you want to come up while I change? It's fourth floor, no elevator."

"Sure. I can handle four floors. Five might be a problem."

The stairs were steep and wound around an ancient wire-enclosed elevator shaft. Ron dashed up, two stairs at a time. When Mel got to the top, he faced an open door, a flat roof, and what was, he supposed, a kind of penthouse with wide windows in the far corner of the roof. Or had it once been a cage for pigeons?

"Originally a playhouse," Ron explained. "That's what they call it, built a long time ago for the owner's children. They don't charge me much for it, and I'm not here a lot anyhow. A friend of mine calls it a shack in the sky. Is that an insult? What's a shack?"

Mel caught his breath while Ron unlocked the door. "I'd say what you've got is better than a shack but not quite a palace. OK?"

Inside, the furniture seemed to have been rescued in its old age just ahead of the trash remover. The bed was unmade. Mel pulled a coverlet over the sheets and sat down. Ron took some clothes out of an old bureau and went into the bathroom to change.

Just as he reappeared, in jeans and a sweater, there was a sharp knock on the door. Ron looked at Mel and shrugged his shoulders. When he opened the door, two gendarmes came in, not hostile, just confident. They said something to Ron. He nodded. The older one looked at his watch and said something more. He pulled some sort of document out of his jacket and held it up for Ron to see. Ron nodded again. He said something in French, and Mel thought he heard the word *American*.

The older gendarme came toward Mel. Mel stood up and waited for the man to say something.

"Be careful, monsieur," the cop said. That was all. The two policemen left as quietly as they had come.

Mel said, "What was that all about?"

Ron said, "Well, they found out about my visa. They know I'm two months late. Illegal."

Mel said, "Oh, I'm sorry."

"And they say I have to be out of Paris by midnight and out of France by noon tomorrow."

"God. That's no time at all."

"I'll get to Brussels tonight. I have a friend there. I'll call him."

Mel hesitated. Then he said, "I'm sorry this happened. Really sorry." He stepped away from the bed. "I guess I should leave. You'll have to pack and everything."

"Yes." They stood silent for a moment. "You can find a taxi."

Mel said, "Is there anything I can do? Anything at all?"

Ron said, "Sure." He held out his arms. "Give me a hug, will you? That's what you call it, isn't it? A hug?"

Mel put his arms around the young man's shoulders and held him for just a moment. Then he whispered in his ear, "God bless you," and turned and left.

**

THE BIG WINNER

I was twelve years old when I climbed the stairs to Ms. Hartwell's apartment for the last time. My weekly piano lessons with this lady, with whom I'd been taking lessons for three years, were going to end that day. Another teacher, Ms. Powell, had arrived in town, easily displaced a long-term organist at the Methodist church, and made herself available for piano lessons.

My mother and her friends were not especially gullible, but they found Ms. Powell irresistible. Her snow-white hair, bright makeup, stylish dresses, and slight British accent reeked of big-city experience, which our local ladies lacked. And Ms. Powell planned to have her students give four recitals a year instead of Ms. Hartwell's single Christmas party.

When my mother heard that the Cantwells were switching their daughter Peggy from Ms. Hartwell to the glamorous Ms. Powell, I knew I would have to switch too. Mrs. Mary Louise Cantwell was a college graduate and bought her clothes in Boston. If anyone knew a good piano teacher when she saw one, Mrs. Cantwell did. She herself did not play, but she had high hopes for Peggy.

My teacher, Ms. Hartwell, lived with her mother on the second floor of a house on Crescent Street. I never knew the people who lived downstairs and presumably owned the house. They always left their front door open as a favor to Ms. Hartwell. I would walk right in that front door and climb the stairs, knock on Ms. Hartwell's door, and wait for her to come open it. The small room with the upright piano had a distinctive smell, which now I imagine came from Ms. Hartwell's mother, who was too frail to even attend church. My parents told me old Mrs. Hartwell had sung in the choir for forty years. The old lady drank eight cups of tea—a mysterious oriental sort—every day. The funny smell could have been the tea.

That day, I decided to take my lesson as if nothing unusual were going to happen. But when we finished, I had to make the statement. That would be my last lesson with Ms. Hartwell. I was going to switch to Ms. Powell. My mother would have made the announcement in person, but Ms. Hartwell did not have a phone, and Mother's bad knee kept her from climbing those steep stairs.

Ms. Hartwell was a thin Yankee lady, not much given to laughter (certainly not giggles) but still kindly and warmly curious about my life away from the piano. When she occasionally played a passage to explain a point, I was greatly impressed. And to hear her talk of Mozart, whose simplest tunes I could stagger through, he seemed her personal friend back in Vienna.

I could not look at her when I said I was leaving. I already had my coat on and my hand on the door, ready for a cowardly escape. But when I was done and turned to say good-bye, she was standing by the piano, silent, smiling, nodding. Her cheeks were wet with tears. I fled down the stairs.

Ms. Powell turned out to be OK. I guess I continued to improve. But when I got to college several years later, I stopped piano lessons. I still played some when I got home for holidays, but many other things took precedence.

In my sophomore year, my mother sent me a clipping from the local paper. At a statewide piano competition that was only held every five years, a student of Ms. Hartwell's, a boy whom I vaguely remembered meeting at my last Christmas recital, had won first prize and a scholarship to Juilliard.

And the best news of all, Ms. Hartwell won Teacher of the Year. I hoped it came with a very large cash prize.

JAILBAIT

"Well. Hi yourself. This is Gary Thompson."

"Wow! A voice from the past. How the hell are you?"

"Couldn't be better. I've just got to tell you something."

"So?"

"Hey. Your voice sounds different. I am talking to Jason Branch, aren't I?"

"You are indeed. I've had a cold. That's all. What a surprise to hear from you. God, how many years ago was it?"

"A couple of centuries, I think. No, seriously, it's just been three years. I was fifteen that summer. You were senior counselor, right? Big chief of the Algonquins."

"What a fucking memory! That's absolutely right. That was my last year at camp."

"You'll be interested to know that I'm chief of the Algonquins this year. I might make universal chief before the summer's over. Did you make universal?"

"No. That asshole Cummins and his Apaches beat us in diving, so he got to be universal, the bastard."

"So now I outrank you."

"Wonderful. Enjoy yourself. Does this mean you're eighteen?"

"Today."

"What the hell? Are you calling from camp?"

"Ever hear of cell phones? Of course I'm calling from camp. At campfire tonight everybody will applaud. For the fourteen-year-olds, eighteen seems like middle age. Want a confession? Since you left camp, I've never much liked it. Know what I mean?"

"Well, sort of. I guess that's very flattering. But you were such a hotshot. If they'd had a piece of wampum for Summer Star Athlete, you'd have won it."

"Well, thanks for the compliment. I'm better now. Three years older and, as they say, three years better."

"Nice going. I really think it's great."

"Want to come to my birthday party tonight? Big fire, lots of marshmallows, all the Coke you can drink."

"Well, I haven't—"

"I know you haven't. But I'll be great eighteen. Helluva lot better than sweet sixteen. The party will be over by seven. The young warriors have to get their sleep. Can't have drowsy braves toppling into the campfire."

"Gee, I'd like—"

"Puh-leeze. We can go back into town later if you want to. I'll be eighteen, for God's sake. You'll have your car."

"Or I could bring my sleeping bag."

"Now you're talking. Remember that great patch of moss over by Moose Hill? It's still there. Remember?"

"Of course I remember. I remember every damn thing about that night."

"O ho. So do I. You were such a law-abiding citizen. So proper. No matter what I did, you acted like you didn't notice. I nearly froze to death running around like that. I couldn't even get you to share a blanket. You know what would have warmed me up?"

"I have my suspicions."

"A hug. A big hug from you."

"I thought about it."

"But nobody'll hug a fifteen-year-old except his mother."

"Not if you want to stay out of jail."

"But now . . ."

"What?"

"I'm eighteen. No longer jailbait. Not in this state. Just want to draw it to your attention."

"Jesus!"

"What's the matter?"

"Are you saying what I think you're saying? If so, you've got more balls than the National League."

"So why don't you bring that double sleeping bag you used to have?"

"Are you serious? Or just pulling my leg? If you're kidding, you're the bastard of all time."

"Three years ago, I knew what you wanted. And I still know."

"And you?"

"Me too. I wanted it—hey, not *it*, I wanted *you*. And now, thank God, I'm eighteen."

"I'm sort of . . . what's the word? Flabbergasted?"

"Are you still the big stud you were a couple years ago?"

"I guess."

"I'll be waiting down at the front gate about five-thirty. Then we can drive up to the lodge together. The boss'll remember you. You'll be the guest of honor. Do you still have that gorgeous ass?"

"Oh, c'mon."

"I hope it's brought a lot of pleasure to the world in the last three years."

"God! Where did you get that filthy mind?"

"OK. A tiny bit of pleasure to the world."

"You win. I've had a couple of compliments."

"Exactly how many?"

"Oh, I dunno. A few."

"Hey, tonight I'll make sure there's an extra hotdog for you. Big chief like big hot dog."

"Gee. You think of everything."

"Hey! This is gonna be the best birthday I ever had. Or maybe ever will have!"

"Two big chiefs making big treaty. And we'll both bring our peace pipes."

"Mine'll be ready."

"Mine too."

"See ya."

THE BRITISH BOY

Good luck is hard to come by. But every once in a while, somebody like Gerard Battles comes along who inspires us all to keep our fingers crossed and our faith unshaken.

Gerard, aged twenty-two, graduated from Reading University, having spent much of his time learning how, more or less, to paint. He identified himself, if asked, as an artist and lived with a friend in a relatively decent flat in the east end of London. His father, a policeman up north in Newcastle, thought he was nuts and frequently shared that opinion with Gerard. His mother insisted he see a doctor when she heard he had charisma. Despite these parental misunderstandings, Gerard was so enthusiastic, so confident, and so electric he seemed to glow with a cheerful aura. It was hard to imagine him failing. His adventures, which he may have actually experienced, were always inspirational and successful.

"It's hard to believe, but just that tiny touch of crimson made all the difference," he said. "When it went up for sale, one of Ben Britten's neighbors in Aldeburgh snapped it up. Just that minuscule spot of red. Amazing! And a good price too, if I do say so."

Friends and parents of his university buddies, some being rather influential, realized that Gerard at a dinner party was as stimulating, and much cheaper, than vintage wines that cost a queen's ransom.

"I only met the prime minister once," he said at one such dinner party. "Purely by chance I assure you. I was having dinner with the parents at La Cocotte. The poor dears'll even eat frogs' legs there if the light is sufficiently dim. And who should come out of the loo but that philistine, John Major. Believe it or not, his flies were open. So of course, I jumped up, acting the part of a great admirer and whispered the startling news in his ear while I gave him a discreet, public-school hug. He was grateful but, of course, didn't hug me back. Not a warm person, I'd say. But I decided I'd done my duty for my country."

At one such get-together, Gerard met the visiting New Yorker, John Bevens, who had just published the best-seller, *Who Remembers Adam and Eve?* On the grounds of his estate in Southampton, Long Island, Bevens ran the Barnyard, originally a large guest house, converted into a studio for young artists who needed a place to work for a couple of summer months. Bevens invited eight each summer, most of them referred by his friends. He invited Gerard, reputed in London to be on the very cutting edge of European painting. Doubtless, Gerard was more sophisticated than the Barnyard's usual contingent of proficient young Americans. Bevens expected the Englishman to spice up the old Barnyard and agreed to pay Gerard's round-trip airfare.

**

Since the Barnyard did not provide living quarters, the young artists were doled out, as Bevens put it, to his friends in the Hamptons, a part of Long Island that virtually glittered during the summer with some big, many small, artistic talents. Bevens had a way of making his friends feel lucky, even blessed, to host a young poet or painter for a whole summer. His offers were turned down only by the terminally ill or suddenly bankrupt. Few were brave enough to take the chance of turning Bevens down, thereby showing up in his next novel faintly disguised and nastily exposed.

"He's a wonderful painter, Hilda," Bevens told Harold McIntosh's wife, Hilda, who, like her husband, was a poet occasionally published in the *New Yorker*. "And such a sweet kid. I can't wait to share him with you. You'll want to adopt him. Never boring. I can't imagine offering him to anyone else."

"Of course we'll take him, lovey," she said. She hoped she'd hidden the lack of enthusiasm in her voice. "Harold's nephew was coming in August, but of course, we can put him off. Would your boy stay all summer? I mean, with us?"

"I hope so, and I'm positive you'll hope so too once you've met him. And I didn't tell you how handsome he is, did I?" Bevens had been on the phone all morning, placing his students. Hard to remember which fibs he had used on which hostesses.

"No you didn't, lovey," she said. She called everyone lovey, a mannerism, she thought, that humanized her and made her more approachable than some other major poets who kept forgetting their best friends' names.

"Well, take my word for it. Handsome as a young Prince Philip. Remember how beautiful he used to be?"

"I wasn't quite born when Elizabeth picked him out of the crowd, lovey," she said, a little white lie. "But it never hurts to have a bit of beauty around the house. God knows we could use some. They say that damned blight is going to hit the rhododendrons again this year."

"You'll adore him, take my word for it. I'd sell my soul for the chance to chat a little longer, but I really must run. Those movie people are coming for lunch. If I don't see you before I bring Gerard over—his name is Gerard Battles by the way, a name the whole country will know someday—have a fine weekend."

"Same to you, lovey. I can't wait to tell McIntosh." She decided to break the news to her husband after he relaxed with a martini that evening. Or perhaps the next day. Or Monday might be even better. Why spoil the weekend?

When the young Englishman was introduced to the McIntoshes, he gave each of them a long, enfolding hug while Bevens stood by, beaming. Harold McIntosh pulled away, astonished. Hilda hadn't realized Brits could be so friendly. And he was attractive in a boyish sort of way. Naturally, his hair was too long.

At the Barnyard, where the students practiced their artistry, he was assigned a sunny corner and a decrepit easel with a rack of paints and brushes. Each of his fellow Barnyarders got a giant hug, some enjoying it less than others. He plunged into his work with ferocious intensity, seldom stepping back to evaluate his work, often passing up lunch, laughing or groaning or snorting in amazement as his current undertaking began to take shape. A nearby rather stout young woman who was painting miniatures the size of postage stamps was unable to make sense of his work, but she was courteous enough to tell him it was striking. She thought she could make out firecrackers and hand grenades in it, but that was only a guess.

"It's antiwar, isn't it?" she said.

"Oh yes, it certainly is. With a pastoral overlay."

"Yes, I see that. And its bigness is important."

"I think so. You feel it, do you?"

"Not influenced by the Barcelona gang, that's for sure."

"Once you've experienced a giant like Titian, it's hard to veer away into the post-moderns."

"Like Robert Frost," she said.

"Exactly. Love his stuff."

**

The McIntoshes, reluctant hosts, survived the British invasion for the whole month of July and then surrendered. McIntosh, who had a phobia about using the phone, insisted his wife solve the problem. He suggested she foist Gerard off on some unsuspecting acquaintance, somebody like Bud Stendhal, the playwright.

"I'm going to make this short, Bud," she said.

He was surprised she remembered his name. "What's your hurry?" the playwright said, "Marlene got fleas again?"

"If I commit murder, I wanted you to be the first to know. This Barnyard kid is driving us both up the wall. Way, way up. He's just like all the others. Crazy as a loon. Please God, you'll take him off our hands. You'd just have to keep him for August."

"I've heard he's rather a handful."

"OK, let me tell you. *Impossible* isn't the word. He's even given Marlene the shakes."

"What is he, by the way? What breed?"

"He's a Brit. Oh, you mean Marlene? He's mixed, lovey. Part Irish setter and part Dalmatian. Maybe a bit of standard poodle. But he's our dream boy, that's what he is."

"I've always thought Marlene was a strange name for a male dog."

"Well, yes. When he was a tiny puppy, we thought he was a girl. And we'd just met Ms. Dietrich over at Bevens's. So the name Marlene seemed heaven-sent. But then a couple of weeks later, we saw she was a boy. McIntosh wanted to change his name to Marlboro, like the cigarette ads. But I don't smoke, and I do worship Ms. Dietrich, so we stuck with Marlene."

"Well, that clears that up. I've wondered for years."

"Nevertheless, lovey, let me explain our problem with the damned Brit. Do you remember that lovely doghouse McIntosh built for Marlene? Very rustic, down on the edge of the woods, a miniature log cabin?"

"I guess so."

"My husband planted the most expensive ivy alongside, and it grew all the way over the roof."

"OK."

"So this bastard from Britain . . . well, I shouldn't say that. He's really quite charming . . . he volunteered to touch up our dear little doghouse. That's what he said. 'Touch up.'"

"And?"

"And he tore off all the ivy, every last shred, and painted Marlene's very favorite building with red and white stripes. Vertical. Like a barber's pole.

Absolutely ghastly. He says it's a triumph. Marlene refuses to step inside. Looks at it and just whines. McIntosh is threatening to give poor Marlene a good kick if he keeps getting in the way. He won't leave the house, the dog, that is. Won't leave our house. Hates his own house."

"Not a problem easily solved. Best of luck."

"But you're young and tough enough to keep our Mr. Expert under control. You really are, lovey. Tell him where to dump his dumb theories. Preferably off a dock in Montauk, but that's just a suggestion. You're still under forty, aren't you? Of course you are. You'll love him. Our trouble is we could be his grandparents. We're not used to kids around, let alone our poor displaced Dalmatian and a damned British basket case. Sometimes he gets talking so hard I think he's having a seizure. Listen, lovey, do this for us, and I'll dedicate a sonnet to you. Tempting?"

"I suppose he's gay."

"That's up to you, dear. Seems everybody is."

"So OK, Here's the deal. I'll take him. But I'll expect two sonnets, one from each of you. Of course, I am trying to write a play, but who cares about that? And frankly, I'm sure you'd tattle on me to Bevens if I turned you down. He's like a mother tiger with those artsy kids."

"How did you know I love to tattle? I'd probably drive over there to tell him face to face. Bevens would poison your name with all his producer friends in the city. And in Hollywood. You could say good-bye to showbiz, don't doubt it for one minute. Lovey, I'd say the rest of your life depends on this decision."

Hilda McIntosh explained to Gerard that they had promised their nephew and his family—wife and four kids—the full month of August. Nephew had a terminal illness, she confided, and probably wouldn't be able to spend a summer vacation with them again, ever. When she saw tears starting to appear in Gerard's eyes, she mercifully added that a doctor at Sloan-Kettering was slightly hopeful. That evening, after Gerard seemed to welcome the move, the McIntoshes toasted each other and heaved a delicious sigh of relief.

**

Bud Stendhal arrived with his ramshackle Ford station wagon to help Gerard move. The first day of August in the Hamptons was considered the beginning of the hottest days of the year. Ocean breezes seemed to have gone on vacation elsewhere. Women appeared in downtown Southampton and Sag Harbor in shockingly revealing outfits. A retired Yale professor wore his Bermuda shorts so far below his belly that a policeman issued him a warning.

The two, small bedrooms at Bud Stendhal's home were air-conditioned. The doors and windows in the rest of the house stayed wide open except during the heaviest rainstorms. Even the rain in August seemed warm.

On the rare afternoon that Gerard wasn't at the Barnyard, he offered to mow the lawn, a small patch between flower beds in back of Stendhal's home. He'd finish in twenty minutes, almost running behind the mower. Then he'd spread out a couple of towels, take off his clothes, and sunbathe. He accomplished the mowing, the flapping towels, and the hurling of himself down onto the ground as if the sun might disappear the next minute. His host figured he mowed the lawn just so he'd have a sweet-smelling place to stretch out. Gerard announced that Stendhal's little place was a suburb of paradise. Stendhal, looking out his study window at Gerard Recumbent, decided that paradise was not entirely lost.

When Stendhal had important contacts in for drinks, Gerard insisted on playing the butler. No uniform, of course, but tight jeans, barefoot, and a Barnyard tee shirt. And invariably, he'd manage to tell a tale of degenerate London aristocrats disporting themselves in the shrubbery behind Buckingham Palace. Or an appalling story about three elderly ladies-in-waiting doing unspeakable things in the royal stables. "The queen insisted on their being burned at the stake, but they escaped to the south of France."

"Cannes, I suppose," some spoilsport sneered.

"Near Juan les Pins, actually. They opened a combination bed-and-breakfast and American-style dude ranch. It took off right from the start. Giant success. Mostly women guests, of course."

"That's the biggest bunch of bull I ever heard."

"Oh, I know it's true," he'd say. "They invited me once. Couldn't go because mater was having her gallstones removed. Very nearly died."

Stendhal at first feared his friends would think these foreign fantasies might influence his own work. Arthur Miller had always been his idol. So he led the chorus demanding, without the slightest success, that Gerard stop lying through his teeth. Then he began to fear these people would think he was too vanilla, too New England, compared to this imaginative British import. So he began inviting people not for dinner but for lunch. At midday, there was little likelihood they'd experience Gerard.

To those people who had grown attached to Gerard, Stendhal would say, "Oh, he'll be so sorry to miss you. But he's a really hard worker. Just doesn't know when to stop. Have a spoonful more of lobster salad." They'd always want to be remembered to adorable Gerard.

**

In the middle of August, the Barnyard held its annual art show under a tent beside the swimming pool at Bevens's palazzo. Of the eight Barnyarders that year, six were painters. Gerard showed a total of eighteen paintings, two of them being five feet square. All of his work juxtaposed startling colors and never condescended to the rendition of actual objects, not a tree, mountain, or coffee cup, or anything even vaguely related to a common man's experience. And eye-catching was too trivial a word for them. Bevens volunteered to a friend that they reminded him of atonal chamber music. A Princeton man said they were like the densest of T. S. Eliot's late poetry.

Nobody offered to buy a Gerard Battles. Bevens considered himself a good judge of value. He decided on the prices to be put on each work, and the young artists were in no position to argue. They were surprised and pleased that he valued their work so highly. But they also couldn't imagine any sane person paying eight hundred dollars for an orange-and-green unframed smear the size of a playing card. Still, compared to Bevens, what did they know about value?

Bud Stendhal chatted with Emily Watkins, who always wore black and would never explain why. She had worked at Fabulous Gardens, a gallery in Wainscott, for a dozen years after graduating from Sarah Lawrence and finally decided to open her own gallery. She had run ads in the East Hampton Star for several weeks. The opening was scheduled for Labor Day weekend. After her third cup of rum punch, she confided to Stendhal that she hadn't the slightest idea whom she was going to show. No one had contacted her. She'd expected to be overwhelmed with begging artists. She was getting panicky.

And then began the conversation that changed Gerard Battles's young life. Emily Watkins thought his work was just indescribable enough, just baffling enough, to draw a crowd. She pointed at all the people crowding under the tent, staring at his paintings. They might show up at her gallery. She would spend big bucks on advertising.

"What do you think?" she said. "Would he do it?"

"My God, he'd be delirious," Stendahl said. "He'd probably have a nervous breakdown."

"Would Bevens come? You know, the author."

"Yes, dear, I know Bevens. That's where we are, even as we speak. We're at Bevens's home right now."

"Oh, sorry," she said, sipping at her drink. "It's so upsetting."

"Of course he'd come," Stendahl said. "He'd claim Gerard was his discovery, his protégé, probably even his lover."

"Oh, is he really?"

"I'm sure I don't know. We mustn't pry. But I do know you'd have a neat little success on your hands, an unforgettable opening. What are you calling the gallery?"

"Are they really sleeping together?"

"Fine. A great title. Don't change a word of it."

**

When Labor Day rolled around, Gerard's paintings were installed on the walls of Emily Watkins's new gallery, cleverly called the Nameless. They were hung rather haphazardly, Stendhal thought, but that was what Gerard wanted. All three of the newspapers in the Hamptons covered the opening, mostly concentrating on the attractiveness of the gallery, carefully skirting judgments of the paintings, commenting merely on their audacity, their storminess, and their rhythm, visual rhythm being a favorite phrase that summer. The *Sag Harbor Express* wrote, "They suggest the waltzes of imperial Vienna under the Hapsburgs, along with a hint of Caribbean calypso drumming."

The reviews did not displease Gerard. "Of course I never read reviews, but these are rather sweet. Not like the bitchery, hell, the butchery you'd find in London. Perhaps I should stay right here, become a Yank, and all that."

At first, Stendhal thought that was a wonderful idea. Having a successful painter as a friendly tenant would help his reputation, which he feared was growing a bit stuffy. Then he remembered he'd promised a play for Thanksgiving, and all he'd done for a month was stare at his lawn and its occasional occupant. So he bit the bullet and said, "I do think an artist is more creative on his own turf. Especially a young artist." Gerard seemed to like being identified as young.

Stendhal was not entirely delighted that Gerard accepted the advice. But it was in the young man's best interest. Gerard planned to fly home to London two days after the opening, leaving an address, of course, where he could be reached if anything wonderful transpired at the Nameless.

But no flying for Gerard. Two hours after the gallery had closed that first evening, well after eleven o'clock, Emily Watkins phoned Stendhal. "Come down here right this minute. And bring Battles. Gerard, that's his name, isn't it?"

"It's almost midnight, dear. Gerard has gone to bed. And me too."

"You stubborn bastard. I don't suppose you'd even get up for Paul Revere. What's the matter? Are you making love?"

"No, dear, I'm not. We're not. You do have a vivid imagination."

"It is your duty to bring Gerard down here this minute. I do not lie."

"So tell me what's up? For God's sake, it's almost midnight."

"Bamberg is here. He wants to meet the artist."

Bamberg was one of America's greatest film directors, right up there with Spielberg and Scorsese. He had a twenty-acre spread on the ocean in Southampton. Stendhal wondered how in the world Bamberg knew about Gerard. He must have been in the crowd that evening. Or perhaps Bevens had spoken to him. This might be Gerard's moment of glory.

"OK," he said. "We'll be there in twenty minutes."

"Make it ten." She hung up.

The Bamberg name shocked Gerard into action. He dressed in the blazer and white flannels he'd worn for the opening. He combed his hair and sprayed breath freshener into his mouth. He looked like a recent Cambridge graduate just visiting from the family estate in Norfolk.

Emily and Bamberg were sitting in the little circle of furniture against the far wall of the gallery, beneath one of Gerard's huge paintings. To Stendhal that night, it looked like a thundercloud had inspired it.

Emily introduced them, managing to get the names straight and properly pronounced.

Stendhal, shaking hands, said, "A pleasure to meet you, Mr. Bamberg."

"Sorry to get you up at this hour," Bamberg said. He was short, middle-aged, plain as a pancake, and wearing a Greek sailor's cap and a rope for a belt. "But I have a proposition."

Emily said, "He's got a wonderful proposition."

"Oh, I don't know how wonderful it is. But I'll lay it out for you. I know you want to get back to bed."

Emily said, "They're just friends, not lovers."

Bamberg said, "I certainly didn't mean—"

Stendhal said, "Of course not. So?"

Bamberg said, "I've just been adding a couple of guest houses down at Oceanside. They're almost finished. Ready for furnishing. The decorators say I should do something dramatic with the artwork. I have some Picasso prints, nothing fancy, and I want to jazz the place up with lots of color. Impress the natives if you know what I mean."

Stendhal didn't think many of the natives were going to be invited into the Bamberg guest houses, but he chuckled obligingly.

Bamberg turned to Gerard. "You're the artist, I gather. Spectacular work. Bevens was right."

"Well, I . . . just some simple ideas . . . fresh, I suppose . . . glad you like them."

"You're very young, aren't you? Over eighteen?"

"I'm twenty-three, sir."

"Past the age of consent, eh? Nice age. You're a good-looking kid too, but I suppose you know it. Done any acting?"

"Just at university."

"You might be good at it. Have to lose the accent, of course."

"Oh, no problem, sir."

"OK." Bamberg glanced up at the thundercloud. His voice turned businesslike. "I'll buy all your stuff. And you'll come along with it, supervise the hanging, stick around until you think it looks right. Might take a couple of weeks, OK? Or maybe a couple of months. What do you say?"

Gerard seemed paralyzed. Then he put his hand on Stendhal's shoulder for support. But he was looking at Bamberg. "Oh, God, yes." He shook his head as if fighting back tears. "Oh yes, sir, it's a deal."

Emily said, "Mr. Bamberg and I have reached an agreement."

Bamberg said, "Let's not talk money. If our boy has any objections, I'm sure we can work something out."

"Of course we can," Gerard said. "Whatever you say will be perfect."

"Careful, kid. I usually have a lot to say." Bamberg winked at him.

"Yes, sir," said Gerard. "I understand." He smiled and nodded.

It was a done deal. Gerard stayed at Oceanside until Christmas, when he flew back to London. But a week later, he landed in Los Angeles, was met by a driver for Bamberg, and moved into a suite at Mountainside, Bamberg's country house outside Santa Barbara.

"He's nuts," his father said.

"Oh, I'm so afraid for him," his mother said.

"I knew he was special," said Bevens.

"He ruined Marlene," Hilda said. "He's never been the same."

"He's a cool number," Stendhal said. "He actually seemed shy at the gallery that night."

"I love him. I really do," said Emily Watson.

And so did the movie-going public. But you already knew that.

POLLY PRODIGY

Her name was Alexandra McQueen, a four-year-old member of a middle-class Boston family. She was as famous early in the new century as the Red Sox or the Patriots. She was entered in The Musical Future contest at the New England Conservatory and beat children twice her age by playing (admittedly with one finger) the first eight measures of Beethoven's Fifth Symphony. A month later at the spelling bee in Cambridge, sponsored by the Harvard Medical School's child psychology department, she spelled *contiguous* on the first try while her opponents, all of kindergarten age, were struggling over *childless*. Both at the conservatory and at Harvard, she won standing ovations even though the audiences were made up of her natural enemies, the parents of her opponents. The mayor of Boston contemplated declaring the first week in June "Alexandra Week." But he decided on "Johnny Damon Week" instead.

Her nickname, bestowed by her proud parents, was Polly.

"My name's Alexandra," the little girl exclaimed. "I'm not Polly?"

Her mother said, "Now, sweetheart, you know the expression 'Polly wanna cracker'?"

"I do not. What does it mean?"

"Well, some parrots can mimic people. They hear things, and then they can say them. Their voices are sort of funny, but you can understand them. When a parrot's owner asks if it wants a cracker, the bird learns to ask the question, and maybe it knows it will get a cracker if it sounds right, sounds like a human being. Polly's a nice name, don't you think? Parrots are very pretty birds."

Alexandra's parents had a good reason for calling her Polly. Many times the little girl had said things no child should even consider saying. For instance, at a spelling bee, an opponent's mother had complained to the judges about incorrect pronunciations. Polly muttered, "That's crap!" That evening, when her father said "that's crap" at the dinner table, her parents glanced at each other and silently vowed to be careful of their language.

A week later, getting ready for bed, Polly showed her dirty hands to her mother. "Where did I get that shit?" she said.

Her mother said, "That's not a nice word, dear."

"No?"

"Well, it's a word, but we don't ever say it in front of people."

"Why?"

"There are lots of words we don't say. You'll learn all about them. Nice little girls stick with nice words, and that will make Mommy very happy."

Polly agreed obediently. But she thought it would be fun to learn more un-nice words.

Her father was a fine source. He was a broker at Caldwell & Titcomb, an up-and-coming firm on Bedford Street which specialized in commodities trading. Most of the brokers, including Polly's father, were under forty, high-strung young bucks, and participants in one of finance's most hectic and potentially bankrupting specialties.

When in the presence of their clients, they appeared stable and gentlemanly. In the office, they screamed like banshees on a binge, cursing the market in highly imaginative terms, and veering toward physical assault on any buddy who led them into nasty miscalculations.

Polly's father tried to curb his tongue at home. But weren't men supposed to relax and be themselves after a grueling day in the salt mines? Couldn't Polly go to bed a bit earlier, leaving time for Mommy and Daddy to be their normal selves?

Of course, Polly could go to bed earlier. Her bedroom was the smallest of the three bedrooms in the condo, the nearest to the living room, and easily reachable in case she had a nightmare or a coughing spell. The door to the living room was condo thin.

What was said in the living room didn't always stay in the living room. From across the hall, Polly could hear everything that was spoken above a whisper. And as the evenings wore on, her parents gave up on whispering. Subjects included the disrespectfulness of the younger brokers, the sumo-wrestler physique of the managing partner, the sexual tendencies of many of the clients, and the undisguised flirtatiousness of rich females. Were you expected to hop into bed with anyone with money to invest? What a damned business! Why hadn't he stuck to dentistry? His father had been a contented dentist.

His generalized irritation extended to Mr. Fowler, the jeweler on Mason Street who had "fixed" his watch. It wasn't fixed by a long shot.

He said to his wife, "You'll be going down there. Isn't Fowler engraving Polly's cup? The one for dancing like Shirley Temple? I always liked 'Good Ship Lollipop' or whatever the hell it was called."

"It should be ready. I'll pick it up. It'll look nice."

"*And* drop off the watch. I'll sue the bastard if he doesn't do it right this time."

"We can put the cup on the mantle. It'll go right in the middle."

Polly listened a little longer and then went to bed. She liked the idea of visiting Mr. Fowler. He engraved all her cups. He seemed to like sharing her victories.

She wasn't old enough to go to school, even a school for prodigies. So she could go shopping with her mother and maybe, if she acted grown up enough, be rewarded with a Hershey bar or another dictionary. She suspected she'd never get another Hershey bar once she was in kindergarten. It might make her fat.

She acted dutifully shy in Mr. Fowler's shop. Her mother liked to say that Polly was shy. Of course, she wasn't, but shy little girls were always in style. She stood right against her mother's leg and held her hand. When Mr. Fowler brought out the newly engraved silver cup, she smiled demurely.

"What do you say to Mr. Fowler, dear?"

Polly said, "Thank you, faggot."

Mr. Fowler instantly turned ashen white. A moment later, the blood boiled up into his face and threatened to boil over. Then he gripped the side of the showcase, apparently to keep from falling.

Polly's mother said, "What a naughty word! I'm ashamed of you! What a terrible thing to say." She picked up the cup and put her husband's watch on the counter.

"I'll take this naughty girl home. Do try to fix the watch."

Mr. Fowler said, "We don't do watches."

"Oh please. I'm so sorry about—"

"We don't do watches. Ever. Sorry. No watches." And he turned away and went into the back room.

Polly trotted along beside her mother as they left the shop. Her mother was yanking her along, not very gently.

"Now your father will have a fit. He'll be very cross."

Polly said, "I'm sorry." Then she said, "Mommy, what's a faggot?"

MISTAKEN IDENTITY

I'm a cop. The FBI likes me, at least the FBI in Buffalo does. Because I don't go around griping about them, though I'll admit they do like to grab the headlines. And I don't kowtow to them. Some cops think the FBI is just about perfect. But I know they're good but just as human as the rest of us. They like the way I react to them. I don't worship.

So whenever they're on a job in Buffalo, they ask if I can work with them. Precinct 8, my home away from home, is most often pretty quiet, so I'm loaned to the FBI without any problem.

Remember the bunch of terrorists discovered in Buffalo? The bureau was responsible for that job. We local boys had our suspicions all along, but we got word from the bureau to let the cell grow a little, and then they would move in. And that's what happened. They asked for me to be assigned to them again.

All I had to do was sit in the room while the agents interrogated the suspects. In case somebody later on complained of illegal pressure, they wanted an outsider like me to witness everything that went on. I can tell you right now that no prisoner was abused. Not a hand was laid on a single one. In fact, they were treated just as if they were local kids caught stealing a candy bar. A couple of them were even allowed to doodle on a pad while being questioned. In court at the prelim hearing, they went right on doodling. And you know what they were doodling? Us!

They had portraits of the lawyers and the judge. And they honored even me with a drawing. Pretty damn good, too. The *Buffalo Banner* got hold of a couple, and there I was on the front page for all to see. Of course they had their own lawyers too and a dozen or so character witnesses, and they all got a real good look at me. Even people on the street recognized me. Famous, right?

Which is why I decided to go away for a while. My wife didn't like the idea, but I told her she wouldn't like finding my dead body on the sidewalk either. I guess I was thinking of that federal incognito program for witnesses who might get killed if the wrong people caught up with them. That's why I headed for Florida. My old buddy, Oscar Jackson, said he'd put me up. He manages a nice little hotel in Vero Beach. He said he'd seen the story on television. I planned to stay a couple of weeks until the case was no longer headlines.

I think you could say Oscar is very prim. We're both forty-two, but he's already been married twice and divorced twice, and if I was married to him, I'd divorce him too. He dresses like some middle-aged fashion model. He runs everything in the hotel himself, down to the way the beds are made and the silverware polished. So he has as much trouble keeping staff as he does wives. I bet he told his wives what perfume to wear and probably typed up instructions on what he liked and didn't like sex-wise. The only time I saw him halfway relaxed was after a couple of drinks. Thank God for vodka, or probably I would have headed back home after just a couple of days.

It was his idea that we go up to Disney World my first Saturday night. Sounded good. I must say I was surprised he was willing to leave the hotel, but the rooms were all booked, and there wasn't much for him to do. We drove up in his Pontiac in the late afternoon. Evenings in Florida are just about as good as it gets. Nice temperature, light breeze, the ocean always nearby. Even palm trees. Not much like Buffalo.

We went into the Kodak exhibit. Huge screen and a lot of special effects, like a bunch of giant rats running right out of the picture, and then you feel their tails whipping the back of your legs. I wonder who thought that one up. When it happened, you could have heard the screams, including Oscar's, all the way to Miami. And we did a couple of other exhibits, all pretty interesting.

They have a little lake, with fountains in it, and about a dozen restaurants, next to one another, in a horseshoe shape surrounding the sides and back of the lake. Each restaurant features food from a different country—China, Germany, France, Turkey—and we decided the Moroccan was for us because we knew nothing about that country except it was actually in Africa, and I guess we were just feeling adventurous. Neither of us had any idea what Moroccan food tasted like.

We had to wait a half hour or so in the bar. Yes, the Moroccans had a bar. I'm not sure if it's legal for them to drink—religiously legal, I mean—but they served whatever you wanted, from scotch on the rocks to fancy-looking pink pineapple concoctions with paper umbrellas stuck in the top. We stayed simple, vodka for both. More than one.

Our table was nice, big enough for two, white tablecloth, and bright glasses and silver. And something I like, really comfortable chairs. The waiters, all Moroccan, wore black pants and white shirts with red fezes on their heads. And the waitress—yes, just one as far as I could see—wore a black skirt and white blouse. That sole female turned out to be our waitress. I'd guess she was in her early twenties, nice looking, her dark hair pulled back from her very light coffee-colored face, a nice figure, and very smiley and anxious to please. Her English didn't sound too confident. She couldn't do much in the way of explaining what the various menu items meant, but we finally ended up with a sort of bean soup and a lamb stew with rice and a good bottle of California red, which tasted rich and sweet after all the vodka. And I remember there was a kind of oriental music playing in the background.

I noticed our waitress didn't hobnob with the waiters. When she wasn't busy with guests, she retired to the kitchen. But the male waiters gathered whenever they could in a tight clump near the door, like teenagers on a street corner at home. They talked among themselves softly, with one eye on their customers in case they were needed. One of them would look at us, whisper to his buddies, and then they'd all turn their eyes onto us. It seemed unlikely they recognized me, but I was a little paranoid at that point. I'm red haired, and maybe they don't have redheads in Morocco. But the way they stared and talked, it seemed they had an unusual lot of curiosity about redheads.

I must admit that by the time we ordered dessert, we'd had plenty to drink. Our lovely young waitress knew her desserts real well and recited them in fairly clear English even though I doubt she understood what she was saying. After all our brave experimenting with unusual food from a faraway continent, we both ordered chocolate ice cream, pure and simple. Yasmin (we finally got up the courage, Dutch courage, to ask her name) hastened off to the kitchen. The waiters were busy at their tables except for the tallest and darkest-skinned one of the bunch, who seemed a bit older, maybe their leader. He continually stared at us even when I stared back. Maybe he was just dreaming with his eyes open, and maybe I was just imagining things, but he made me nervous.

Yasmin came back with the ice cream. She leaned over to put it down, but the table was still covered with our dirty dinner dishes.

Oscar looked up at her with a heavy frown. "They should teach you to clear the table before serving another dish." He gestured at our dirty plates.

"It is not well mannered to serve chocolate ice cream in the midst of dirty stew dishes. Understand?"

Which is when all hell broke loose. Yasmin uttered a tiny shriek, tears gushed from her eyes, and she dropped both dishes of ice cream onto the floor and fled sobbing into the kitchen. As the kitchen door closed behind her, I heard a heavy thump that I knew to be the sound of a body falling to the floor.

Oscar said, his eyes bulging, "I was just trying to teach her."

The clump of waiters stood still as statues, eyes focused on our table. The entire restaurant was silent. The tall dark waiter suddenly looked familiar. Did I know him from Buffalo?

Two of the younger waiters hurried toward us. I stood up, ready for whatever was coming.

One of them said, "No, no, no. Not to worry. Everybody sorry. She brand new. So sorry." The other tried to spoon up the fallen ice cream.

I said, "I'm awfully sorry. My friend was just explaining something to her."

"It's all right. She new. Very sorry."

I glanced toward the waiters' gathering spot. The tall dark one held a cell phone to his ear and was talking into it. And staring at us.

The waiter with us said, "She'll be all right. Her husband look after her."

Oscar said, "Her husband?" I could see thoughts of a husband's revenge bubbling through his brain. A razor-sharp Moroccan sword. A thin wire around the neck from behind.

Our waiter pointed. "That's her husband. Married three weeks." He was pointing at the tall dark one, who still stood glaring by the door.

"Oh God, oh God," Oscar breathed. He said to the waiter, "Can you please get us our check? Quickly, please."

"Take it easy," I said to Oscar. "We'll get out as soon as we can."

The tall dark man left his post. He headed in our direction.

Oscar saw him coming. He said, "That one's no Moroccan. He looks like an Arab, doesn't he?"

Oscar had asked me very little about my Buffalo terrorists. I knew he was not trying to frighten me. He was sweating and mopping at his face with a napkin.

I was the one that should have been sweating. The Arab was not going to attack Oscar. Perhaps he was going to pull a picture out of his pocket and ask me if I was the man. Or maybe he'd just pull out a gun and get it over with.

Instead, he walked right past us and on into the kitchen. When the door swung open, I could hear a woman crying from a long way off. I suppose it was Yasmin. Was being asked to clear the dishes an unbearable, unspeakable insult in Morocco?

Then two things happened at almost exactly the same time. Our waiter returned with the bill. Oscar pulled out a wad of cash and hastily peeled off several twenties.

"Please keep the change," he said. "Thank you very much."

And then the police arrived. Two of them. I knew from the uniforms they were employees of the park, not real city police. They stood for a moment in the doorway. Our tall dark terrorist pushed in behind them. He must have exited through the kitchen. He pointed at us. The officers headed for our table.

One said, "You've been harassing a waitress."

The other said, "You're coming with us."

I said, "I'm a police officer. We haven't been harassing anybody. I swear."

Oscar said, "Oh my God."

The first officer said, "You're out of here right now. Understand?"

Oscar said, "Of course. We're out of here. Right now."

And so, that late Saturday night, the officers walked a few paces with us away from the Moroccan restaurant.

Then they stopped, extended their hands, smiled, and said, "Welcome. Sorry for the confusion." I smiled back but didn't know what to say. Oscar just stood there.

Then one of them said, "Them damned Mexicans get hysterical if you just look at them."

"Mexicans?" I said.

"Hell, you don't think they'd waste money on real Moroccans, do you? I'm more Moroccan than them phoney illegals in there. Now one of them's got a cell phone. Probably stole it."

**

The wonderful Florida air wasn't smelling quite so sweet that evening. The moon was looking rather misty. The palm trees definitely looked awkward. As we walked back to the car, Oscar muttered, "Jesus!"

I said, "Between us, I'll take Mexicans over Moroccans any day. But that's not fair. I've never met a Moroccan. Maybe they're terrific."

We didn't talk much on the way home. In fact, I managed to fall asleep.

CHALLENGE

"Hey, you can go six months with nothing but baptisms and lost dogs." The editor laughed. "Sometimes a year or more. And then all of a sudden you've got a murder. You just have to be ready for the big story when it comes along. Or should I say if it comes along."

Will already knew that journalism was no steady job. It was an unsteady job, and maybe that's why he loved it.

He was twenty-eight, single, and a graduate of Dartmouth with a degree in journalism from Columbia. Then two years in the army, including time overseas as a liaison with the Afghan press.

With his honorable discharge and academic credentials, he had no trouble landing a job on the *Fairmont Express*, which had the largest circulation of any daily in Vermont. He tried to act interested, even appreciative, when his editor, usually after what he called a damp lunch, launched into a lecture on the meaning and practice of journalism.

At the *Express* there was no such title as crime reporter. But he managed to cover the rare burglary, the drunk-driving arrests, and the fights between summer tourists and young locals, the disagreement usually involving the sexiness and availability, or lack thereof, attributed to certain young ladies.

There had been no murder in that part of Vermont since the late '70s. Nor had there been a suicide except for the old lady who gassed herself in her kitchen when told she had inoperable brain cancer. That had caused a real flap, her doctor being blamed, and her absent children reviled. Will had hardly been born when that tragedy occurred.

He was six months on the job when Jon Paulsen committed suicide. The town of Fairmont was horrified. Jon was seventeen, about to graduate from High School, and a fine student headed for Cornell.

Will's editor said, "I'm not sure suicide is a crime, but you wanted to cover crime, so why don't you take this one."

"Good deal," said Will. "More than just an obit, right?"

"We'll do the obit tomorrow, but I want a story for Friday. The whole town's pretty upset."

"I gather he was quite a star."

"He was a kid with a hell of a handicap, that's what he was. A birth defect. A withered left arm, a hand with only a thumb, and no other fingers. But became a decent athlete, I guess mainly in track. And a good enough student to get into college. Talk to his parents. Find out why they think he did it. His father is a real estate agent. A bit holier-than-thou, if you know what I mean, but a decent enough guy. His mother doesn't work."

"Any brothers or sisters?"

"I'm not sure. Talk to them, of course, if there are any."

Will thought of the wartime amputees he had known in Kabul, who grimly accepted their mutilations. No histrionics, no accusations. Just a kind of stalwart acceptance. Not one suicide, not even attempted. What sort of horror had infected this boy? Why was this gorgeous month of May not a potent antidote. Seventeen was supposed to be a yearlong spring day. But this boy had killed himself, hung himself in the cellar, without a word of explanation.

**

The Paulsens had a nice-enough house, nothing fancy but as respectable as its neighbors. A front porch, two storeys and an attic, gray clapboard with white window trim, and a garage that could have used a coat of paint. Each house on the block stood on a quarter acre.

Will decided not to phone ahead. Just showing up might be insensitive, but he had to start somewhere, whether people liked it or not.

A tall young girl, probably fourteen or fifteen, answered the door. She looked tired. Straight blond hair, steady eyes, no smile, blue jeans, and a man's shirt.

"Mom doesn't want any visitors. I'll tell her you were here."

"Are you her daughter?"

"Yes."

"She must be awfully torn up."

"She hasn't slept for two nights."

"Your father isn't here, is he?"

"He won't talk to you either. Does he know you?"

"No. I work for the *Express*."

"Oh God. They sure don't want any publicity."

"I understand. Is there anybody I can talk to? Could you give me a minute?"

The girl hesitated for a moment. "Talk to my grandmother. She lives down at the inn."

"Is she a Paulsen, too?"

"Yes, Dad's mother."

"You think she'll talk to me?"

"Oh, you'll see. She'll talk as much as you want. Jon spent a lot of time with her. He got along with her better than with Dad. Or I guess with Mother."

"Did he get along with you?"

"Oh sure." Her lips pressed together. She started to close the door. "Thanks for coming by."

"Just one more thing," Will said. "How were things at school?"

"He's a senior. He was a senior. I'm a sophomore, so I didn't see much of him. But I think everybody liked him. He was vice president of his class. And on the honor roll. He got into Cornell."

"It's a hard question to ask, but was he awfully bothered by his handicap?"

"You mean his hand?"

"Yes."

"God, I don't know. Wouldn't you be bothered? I would." She nodded to him. "Thanks for coming by." And she closed the door.

**

When Will got to the Downtown Bar & Lounge, his boss was already there. They ordered the hamburger and Coke special and shared an order of fries.

"So you went to the house. Anybody home?"

"I talked to the sister. She said her parents were too torn up to talk. Didn't want any publicity."

"Understandable."

"I didn't learn a damn thing. She said he was upset, or maybe she said he was sorry about his hand, but I got the impression she didn't think that was why he killed himself. By this time in his life, he must have gotten pretty used to it."

"So what was it?"

"If I knew, I'd be a happier man."

"Any chance of finding out?"

"The girl said her grandmother would talk to me. Any information about the grandmother?"

"Oh sure. I've met her a couple of times. Great lady. No bull. Tries to make people think she's a wild-eyed feminist, but I have the feeling she's really a pussycat. Still, she strikes me as a helluva lot gutsier than her son, Jon's father. Travels a lot. Probably has a good deal of money. Has a little suite down at the hotel. She's a smart cookie."

"They're turning out to be quite a family."

The editor sipped at his Coke. "And I don't want to print some garish story about their boy's death just for the sake of a story. If there's no story, we'll just do a good obit, and that'll be the end of it. OK?"

"And if there is a story? If we find out what was eating the kid?"

"Fine. We'll see what it was, and then we'll decide to run it or not run it. Simple."

"Well, I'll let you know if I strike gold."

"Say hello for me."

"Sure."

**

The clerk said, "She's in 201 and 203. Knock on 201. That's her living room. 203's a bedroom. Want me to give her a ring?"

"I don't think you have to. She's up there, isn't she?"

"Oh yeah. We've been sending up meals. That grandson of hers was a terrific kid. I'd like to have a grandson like that someday. Great sense of humor. Always called me Jeeves, whoever the hell that was. She thought the world of him. Terrible thing."

"Terrible thing," Will said.

Mrs. Paulsen's rooms were right across from the rattling old elevator. The hallway smelled dusty, somehow sour. The carpeting was worn. Will wondered how many years, how many decades, had gone by since the last renovation. Probably nothing since the Second World War.

He knocked.

"Oh, hello," she said. "What can I do for you?" She had those unflinching eyes like her granddaughter's. She looked amazingly fit, like the golfing ladies on the senior tour who at fifty still swing a mean driver. Her hair was gray and cut short. She was wearing some sort of ankle-length, brightly flowered Hawaiian mumu. She was barefoot.

"I'm Will Binder," he said. "I'm with the *Express.*"

"Aha. A reporter. I suppose it's about Jon."

"Could you give me a couple of minutes?"

She stepped back and pulled the door open. "Sure, why not."

The room had one antique table and a sofa with a heavily carved back. The rest of the furniture, including the desk in front of a window, was functional but hardly noteworthy. A bright oriental rug and several watercolors had been saved, Will assumed, from the former house, where this confident lady had raised her family.

She said, "He was a wonderful kid." She sat beside the desk and gestured Will to the sofa. "Is that what you wanted to know?"

"Something like that," Will said. "Your granddaughter said you might tell me a bit about him."

"Betsy's a good girl. Not at all like Jon, but they were still real close. Thank God they got along. His parents were pretty difficult. I suppose they wouldn't talk to you." She pointed at a bowl of grapes. "If you like grapes, help yourself. They're better than smoking."

He took one. Mrs. Paulsen reminded him of some lady politician he couldn't quite place, perhaps one who had risen to cabinet level, one who could handle herself with cool confidence before the toughest Senate committee. He respected her. He thought if he knew her better, he would probably like her.

She said, "You know, for your whole life something like this is, well, somebody else. Then the phone rings, and . . ." She ran her hand through her hair. "Did you learn much from Betsy?"

"Can't say that I did."

"Not surprising. She's been sworn to secrecy. He tried to get me to swear too."

"Secrecy?"

"Yes, secrecy. Have you talked to Dr. Tomlinson?"

"Was he Jon's doctor?"

"Our family doctor for years. Older than I am, poor bastard. But still a good doctor. A good friend."

"Would it be a good idea for me to check him out? Doctors aren't supposed to talk about their patients."

"I guess you wouldn't learn much. Whenever Jon got depressed, I made him go see old Tomlinson. He'd go for a couple of months, maybe once a week, and then he'd feel better. People thought he was just going for his hand."

"But . . . ?"

"Tomlinson is no psychiatrist, but he's wise, been around the block a couple of times. Of course, I'm prejudiced. The old coot wanted to marry me once. But he understood when I told him one man in my life was plenty. Probably more than enough. He took to Jon right from the beginning. Just as if he was the kid's grandfather. I think Jon loved him. I guess not enough."

"So why did Jon throw in the towel this time?"

She studied her clasped hands for a moment. Then she looked him straight in the eye. "Because his father, my son, was going to send the poor kid to some god-awful place down in Kentucky. I guess you'd call it a sort of rehab center. Know what that is?"

"Well, more or less. Yes."

"A month ago, I decided to go down and check it out. I'd say it's half like a school and half like a prison. A big brick building, but a very high fence topped with barbed wire, and a dozen guards walking around. Sort of scary. When I got there, the gate was open, but when I drove in, a siren went off, and two men jumped out of the front door like I was going to bomb the place. I should have. The place should be bombed. I'd do it if I could lay my hands on a bomb. I suppose I'm kidding, but the world would be a better place."

"What is it, a college?"

"I'll tell you what it is. It's a place of torture camouflaged as a place of persuasion. The director, or whatever he was, agreed to see me. I said I was thinking of sending my grandson. The poor fool fell for it. God, he was obnoxious. They think they can change a person's very nature. If a kid doesn't see how Jesus could rise from the dead, he'll sure see after two weeks at that hellhole. If a violin prodigy wants to go to New York to study, she'll learn it's better to forget the violin and marry and have kids in Louisville. Mostly young people, of course. Kids whose parents don't like them. This director told me all his grand success stories. I was ready to throw up, so help me. He told me a half dozen electric-shock treatments would cure anybody of anything. When I got back to the airport, I had a little cry. Made me feel better."

"Was Jon supposed to forget his hand? The place sure couldn't give him a new one. They couldn't promise that."

"OK. It's a deep dark secret in the Paulsen family, so please don't print this. Jon told me he was gay. Promise not to print it. Betsy knew. And he confessed to his parents if that's the right word. They'd kill me if they knew I'd talked to you. But I hope you understand."

"We won't print it."

"He loved this kid in his class, and the beautiful thing was the kid loved him back. Doesn't that break your heart? It does mine. And his father, my own son, was shipping him off to be cured. Of course, the boy fought it. He got Dr. Tomlinson to talk to his folks. I'm sure you've guessed: all those sessions with Tomlinson were about being gay, not about his hand. When you're just a teenager and discover something like that, it must be ghastly to cope with. Can you imagine how awful the future looked to him, near-term and long-term?"

"Even Dr. Tomlinson couldn't talk them out of sending him away?"

"Said they were not going to have a fairy in the house. Those were their very words. Betsy said she'd run away if they did that to him. And I think she would too. I told her she could move in with me. I'd get a room for her. Maybe she'll take me up on it."

She stood up. "So that's it," she said. "Betsy might have told you, just to get even. Maybe I'm getting a little bit even too. But I wanted you to get the story straight. So now the press has got hold of it, the almighty American press." She went to open the door. "We're quite a species, aren't we, us humans? If our ignorance doesn't cripple the kids at home, we send them off to be killed in war?" She shook her head, and her eyes were moist. "Remember, you promised not to print it, young man. Don't forget, you promised."

Will stepped into the hallway and turned to shake hands with her.

"Oh," she said. "Let me give you a good laugh. You know what they call that place, that rehab center? They call it Challenge. Can you believe it? I wonder if the challenge is to cure the kids or for the kids to survive. Anyway, glad to meet you."

**

Will reported to his editor. "I promised to keep it all a secret."

"So we shouldn't even say 'a source who prefers to remain anonymous'?"

"Nobody's anonymous on this story. Not in this town."

"Just kidding. We won't say anything."

"I can't help thinking of the bind the kid found himself in," Will said. "If people knew he was gay, they'd put two and two together about his friend. He'd be unintentionally betraying somebody he loved. They'd get at his sister too. Rub salt in the wound. His parents would have to make up some story about his going away for a while, visiting a relative. And he himself would be at that rehab place, which will 'cure' him of being gay. That is, if it doesn't kill him. I wonder how many kids that place actually does kill. A boy Jon's age doesn't have many options. So suicide. Wonderful."

"We'll just run an obit, right? No big story. Nothing about the rehab center."

"No big story about Jon Paulsen, that's for sure."

The editor said, "You got some other story up your sleeve?"

Will said, "Kentucky is a long way from Fairmont, but I'd love to make a stab at exposing that place. By the way, it's called Challenge. Sort of a misleading name, no? We wouldn't have to mention Jon or the Paulsens. Only his family would see the connection."

The editor stared out the window. "I wonder if the senior Mrs. Paulsen would help you."

"Yes she would. I'm sure of it."

"Listen, ole buddy," the editor said. "You better sleep on it. If you take this on, it sure won't be a walk in the park. People have been lynched down there for a lot less."

"Well, I managed to survive the Taliban, so I guess I'm bulletproof. But I'm beginning to think that's not the point. If you'll excuse the expression, I think that place is sinful. Sound like Mr. Goody Two-Shoes, don't I? Well, if I have a chance to do a little good I shouldn't pass it up. It just turns me on a bit more than a story about a flat tire on Main Street."

"Of course I understand. The place makes me want to go crusading too. But if I got into trouble, it would upset the family. At least, I hope it would. But you're still single, so if you're found floating in the Challenge fishpond, who's going to care?"

"Exactly. You're absolutely right."

"But don't even bring up the subject for a couple of days. Let it sink in, or should I say see if it rises to the level of action."

"Promise."

"Maybe if someday you write a juicy enough story about Challenge, you'll get a Pulitzer Prize. Sound good?"

"Hey, now you're talking. Forget the sin angle. I'm going for that gold statue on my mantle piece."

"Just as I suspected. You're a real reporter, kid."

Will smiled and saluted. "See you in the morning."

LETTER FROM HOME

Philip C. Schmidt
Ritz Hotel
Singapore

Dear Phil,

How's the vacation going? You really deserve one, but we miss you and hope you'll be back soon. I hate to interfere with your time off, but I bet you've seen the "funny" articles about the company—it seems every paper and TV station in the world picked it up—and I want to explain exactly what happened. So at least you and I, as cofounders, can tell the same story. And don't for a minute think it's an untrue story. Let me just tell you, as they say, the facts.

Sarah Jenkins was hired three years ago next month. Her husband, who used to be an accountant at Fosdick, had died a while back, and her daughter married a guy from New Hampshire. So I think Sarah told us she just wanted something to do. She had worked on and off at Planx, doing something boring on their assembly line, and she told me she wanted something more "varied" that would take her mind off her troubles. We assumed her "troubles" were the loss of her husband, daughter moving away, and maybe some money problems. As far as I know, those were the only "troubles" she had. No drinking problems or anything like that. Of course, she was almost sixty and overweight, but those are "troubles" we all have, no?

We had an opening in Wiring and Soldering. She understood that it wasn't a huge change from Planx, but it was the only thing we could offer just then. She had worked in Laminates and Finishes at Planx, and what we offered was at least a change. So she took the job.

You remember Sandy Blackwell, don't you? Been with us almost from the beginning. Totally trustworthy. I've asked her a dozen times in the past to "indoctrinate" new employees, and there's never been anything like a complaint. Sandy graduated from Benson High a couple of years before Sarah, and they knew each other vaguely, and it seemed they were a match made in heaven—and of course, I'm just speaking from a corporate point of view. I saw them more than once eating their lunch together out on the back lawn. It never crossed my mind Sarah was under any unusual tension.

Of course, now to hear her talk, you'd think we stood over the girls in W&S with a bullwhip. They know as well as you and I do that a certain number of pieces must come off the line every day—sometimes every hour when we're in a bind—but in our twenty-five years, we never had an accident like Sarah's. And she was there for three years and had plenty of friends. And was good at her job.

Some of the newspapers claim she stuck two fingers into her solder pot. Actually it was only one—the middle finger on her right hand. Of course, the burn was awful. We never denied that. And we agreed to consider the finger, for insurance purposes, a case of digital dismemberment. (That was a new one for me!) Sandy Blackwell drove her to the hospital, and Sarah stayed for three days. The finger never grew back much flesh, but it didn't look too bad, and of course, we gave her back her job.

We made a standard report to the County Health and Safety Office, which we do every quarter, as you know. Thirty-three days later (yes, I was very surprised to hear from them that late) they said they'd send an inspector down to check out the Wiring and Soldering line. It turned out to be a man named Kravitz, pleasant enough, but acting a bit superior like most bureaucrats. Wore a black suit and, with a different collar, could have been a priest.

He knew how much insurance Sarah got, and we told him how many of Sarah's friends from the company had taken her food and kept in touch on the phone. Since Sandy Blackwell was such a good friend, I didn't see any reason why I should bother Sarah while she convalesced. Yes, she even collected money from the county while she "convalesced." You'd think she lost a leg!

She had been back for six working days when Kravitz came for his inspection. He decided to check out the whole factory while he was there. Fine by me. I'm glad to say we have nothing to hide. He ended up at the Wiring and Soldering line, which was working on that Hapgood Motor project. Everybody pretty busy. Kravitz asked me which one was Sarah. I pointed her out. He strolled over to her, patted her shoulder, and I guess he asked her to tell him exactly what happened. So she stuck her finger back into the solder pot. Can you believe it?

She and Kravitz screamed. Then the rest of the girls screamed. Then I almost screamed. Then the screaming turned to sobbing, and good old Sandy Blackwell pushed past Kravitz and took Sarah out. They went to the hospital. Sarah now has not one but two stripped fingers.

So those are the facts. A couple of papers have said I shouldn't be in charge of female employees because I'm a man. Well, I think Henry Ford had some female employees and nobody complained! And I'm white, and some of the girls are black. True enough. Not much I can do about that. Not much I want to do about that. And I'm accused of having a college degree, and they're all high school graduates. The level of education in this company is considerably above other factories in Arkansas.

So that's the story, Phil. Sorry to burden you with this, but I don't want some reporter to blindside you. When you get back, we can figure out a way to keep this from happening again though I'm not sure we should make many changes. This accident never happened to anyone else in twenty-five years.

Sarah has decided not to come back to work for us. Under the circumstances, I think that's just as well.

Best to Mary,
Dan

LUCKY TOBY LANGERFELD

Henry Wedge almost turned down the invitation to address the Boston Bankers' Association. "It's not going to do me any good. It's just fluff."

I knew after ten years that Henry did not like being contradicted. But I said, "You could use a nice long weekend in Beantown. You've been working like a madman. Us old dogs should enjoy life a little."

He began to come around. "I know New York law, but I've never claimed to know anything about Massachusetts."

"I don't imagine they'll expect you to lecture on the law. They'll want to know how to become one of the big bankers of the world."

"Yeah, flatterer. Are banking laws different in Massachusetts?"

"I don't know. I'll find out. When do they want you?"

"Friday, May 22. At a dinner for somebody. I'd be the guest speaker."

"Give me a couple of days. I'll get back to you."

In the decade I had worked for him, I had grown fond of Henry Wedge. He was in his midsixties and still trim as he must have been as captain of the Yale track team. But with considerably less hair and, I suspected, a heart problem that he rarely discussed. On the plus side, he now had a little more patience with his fellow man, a little mellowing around the edges. He had started as an assistant vice president at the bank and, after a lifetime of hoisting himself up the corporate ladder, was now vice-chairman. He told me once he would like to have been offered a job at Treasury, but the phone never rang.

"They think I'm a dictatorial bastard, don't they? A modern-day Mussolini."

"They know you had to be tough to get to the top."

"I am not dictatorial. I just expect people to do the jobs they're paid to do."

"No arguing with that."

He said Boston hadn't changed. Still a cold, lonely city. The speech went well. He got a standing ovation. Besides the bankers, he met a few politicians and a professor from Harvard Law. About a hundred people, including, he told me, Toby Langerfeld, a twenty-year-old assistant in commercial loans. Toby had graduated in accounting from Waltham Community College eight months earlier. His parents were proud.

"How the hell did you meet this Toby?" I asked. I hoped it wasn't at the baths or some grungy bar where he might have been recognized. It crossed my mind that as Henry grew older, the more contradictory he became. He indulged himself with food, drink, sex, and every imaginable entertainment but at the same time expected people to believe he lived like a monk.

He told me that after the speech, he stood in front of the lectern to shake hands with the guests. He was tired and ready to leave. When Toby Langerfeld, blond, blue-eyed, and grinning, appeared, Henry Wedge instantly felt better. He remembered every word of that meeting. He quoted it to me verbatim.

"And you are?"

"Langerfeld, sir. They call me Lucky Langerfeld. Commercial loans. A good speech. I learned a lot."

"Well, I hope it was entertaining as well as educational."

"I never heard the one about the med school student. Brought down the house, didn't it?"

"Old as the hills. But I guess nobody's told it for twenty years. Let it marinate, as they say."

"Are you going back to New York tonight? A long trip."

"I'm used to it. I could get a good night's sleep in a wheelbarrow if I had to. Luckily the bank insists I use a Cadillac."

For good reason, Henry Wedge had never been offered a job in Washington. Clearly, he could be nasty at times and famously intolerant of people less competent than himself. Once, a Brooklyn woman who had been his housekeeper for three years sued for breach of contract. He had fired her because she arrived late for work four mornings in a row. Happily, I saw to it that the suit was quickly dismissed.

No president had ever invited Henry to Washington for one simple reason. He was gay. Both his marriages ended in divorce, both ladies receiving handsome settlements and neither one revealing Henry's sexual proclivity. In those marriage years, he was extremely discreet. Otherwise, the bank would have fired him. I wondered, during those divorces, why he decided to confide in me. I think he considered me a sort of insurance. In case he ever got in trouble, it would be good to have a lawyer on tap, one who did not work for the bank. But he avoided trouble, never seemed stressed by anything outside the bank, always maintained his abrasive and cocksure approach to life. His monthlong summer vacations were spent totally incommunicado in Rio or Bangkok or Amsterdam. Those vacations seemed to satisfy his secret needs, as far as I knew, for the next eleven months.

And then he met Toby Langerfeld.

**

I was sure after my first dinner with the two of them that Toby was not, as Henry sometimes suggested to others, a distant cousin trying to decide on a career. The young man seemed to thoroughly enjoy living in Henry's Fifth Avenue apartment with its oriental rugs, three Degas oils, and view of Central Park. He probably saw himself living there the rest of his life. I never figured out how he spent his days. Henry referred vaguely to Toby's studies.

"He's thinking of Wall Street, but I'm trying to dissuade him."

"I'm an accountant," Toby said. "They must need accountants on Wall Street."

I said, "Take your time. Don't waste a couple of years on something that doesn't turn you on." I knew neither of them would listen to me, but I thought Toby deserved some unbiased advice.

"Henry doesn't want me to go into finance, do you?"

"I don't think you're cut out for it, that's all. It's too cold, too straight-laced. Not much room for creativity."

"You think I'm creative?"

A question that struck them both as hilarious. Henry put down his fork and mopped at his lips. Toby, chuckling, looked back and forth between Henry and me as if he expected Henry to explain the joke to me. I knew from Henry's reaction it was unlikely he would offer an explanation. Whatever *creative* meant to them, I could only guess. The meaning must have been loaded with emotion.

But that evening, as he was seeing me out, Henry followed me into the hall. "For your information, the word *creative* came up a couple of nights ago. I told him he was being very creative. He does things I didn't know could be done. Never been done by me or to me. He says I should get out more, learn some new techniques. That's all. If I ever get drunk with you again, I'll give you all the steamy details."

A year later, Henry told me he was going to change his will. He came to my office. He was anxious to get the papers signed, sealed, and delivered.

He left his estate to Toby, minus token donations to Yale and the Red Cross. Toby would be a very rich young man. I said I would have it ready for his signature in two weeks. I would bring my secretary with me, to act as one of the witnesses, and Toby could be the other.

Right on schedule, Mrs. Severn and I arrived at the apartment. The doorman announced us over the intercom. Toby answered the door. He was so drunk he could hardly keep his balance. I hadn't seen him for months. In that time, he had lost some of his youthful glow. He was still handsome, but not quite the young god he had been. He didn't look directly at me or offer to shake hands with Mrs. Severn. His clothes seemed shabby. He was barefoot. He gestured us toward Henry's study.

Henry greeted us, suggested we sit down while he handled one little chore. When he came back, he told us Toby was taking a shower. We made small talk, mostly about Degas, a favorite of Mrs. Severn's.

The young man finally came in, his hair wet and combed, his face shiny red, wearing new clothes. The papers were quickly signed, and we left. I knew Mrs. Severn would eventually want to know a little more about Toby Langerfeld, whose name had seldom come up at the office. I hoped I would be inspired to tell a vague but believable tale that would satisfy her.

I had no way of knowing if Toby had always been a drinker. It was possible he did his drinking during the day and sobered up in the evening for Henry's return. God knows he was playing with fire. No one ever claimed that Henry was tolerant of other people's weaknesses. One TV anchor laughingly referred to him as the Butcher. Our receptionist would announce his arrival at the office as "the Axman cometh." With me, of course, he was always civil. We considered ourselves friends.

Another six months went by before the subject of Toby came up again. Henry asked me to dinner at the Plaza, halfway between our apartments. Toby was not included. I wondered how often the two of them appeared in public together.

Once dinner and drinks were ordered, Henry said, "He's fallen in love with somebody else."

"Oh wow. I'm sorry."

"A boy from ABT. American Ballet Theater. Named Carlo."

"Have you met him?"

"No. Seen him but not met him. Gorgeous kid, I'll admit. Hard to believe Toby'd do this." He tried to pick his words carefully. It would never do for Henry Wedge to reveal a sentimental streak. "It went on for a couple of months before I suspected anything. Unpleasant finding yourself blindsided at my age." He had never admitted any sort of weakness to me before. Nor, I'm sure, to anyone else.

"Well, at least you finally wised up. Some people never do."

"You know he turned into a drinker. Really bad. Never took one job interview in two years. Said he had nothing to offer. Who would want him? He was right, as far as I could see. Blotto every day."

"He didn't blame you, did he? Didn't say you drove him to it?"

"Never. Hell, he wouldn't dare. Actually, I thought he liked living with me. It sure beat Waltham, Massachusetts. At least I suppose it did. Then it all went sour. He's moved into some dump in Brooklyn with this Carlo." He pushed his coffee cup away. "I'll have to do something. I'll let you know."

**

Within a week, Henry told me to change his will. He came to the office to sign it. Almost everything to Yale, a bit for charity, and no mention of Toby Langerfeld. When I warned that Toby might raise a stink, Henry said, "Hell, I'm going to outlive that ungrateful bastard. Believe me. Anyway, he wouldn't know how to raise a stink. Not the brightest kid in the world."

But that ungrateful bastard didn't call Henry. He called me. His language was slurred. It was two in the afternoon, and he was undoubtedly drunk.

"You got a minute?" he asked.

"Sure. What can I do for you?"

"Here's my address if anything comes in. 1209 Bowker Street in Brooklyn. I think the zip is 10335. No phone. Isn't that a gas? How the mighty have fallen. I'm in a phone booth."

"I'm not sure any mail for you would be sent to me. Henry's building would handle it."

"No they wouldn't. He'd make sure of that. He won't even answer his phone. No good dealing with Henry. Never was any good. You're his buddy, but you don't know what a pig he is. There's Henry's way or no way. He used to try to beat me up, you know."

"No, I didn't. And I think *pig* is a bit harsh."

"But what about me? I almost went nuts. Instead I had a drink or two. That's how you get along with Henry. Carlo says I should sue him. But Carlo doesn't know anything. He's only been here a year, and he's going back to Brazil. But you know what? Now I can say I've been in love with someone my own age. I think we all deserve to have one affair like that, don't you?"

I suppose he was right. But I said, "And you'll be heading for Boston?"

"They won't have me. They say I'm a lush. And a queer. All washed up at twenty-four."

"I'm sorry, Toby. Very sorry. But there's not much I can do. I can just wish you good luck."

"Would you help me see Henry?"

"That's not possible, I'm afraid."

"Do you think he would help me?"

"He's not in a very helping mood. You know he had a stroke."

"Jesus. No."

"A week ago. I saw him the day before."

"Did he want to . . . I mean, did he shut me out of his will?"

"I shouldn't tell you, but yes he did."

"Should I go see him?"

"They won't let you in. He's at Lenox Hill. He's in a coma."

"So that's the end of me I guess."

"I certainly hope not."

"He must think he really got even."

"I don't know what he thinks, Toby. He's not expected to live."

"OK. Thanks for the time. Sorry I bothered you."

"No bother. And like I said, good luck."

"Yeah. Thanks."

In less than a week, Henry Wedge died. There's a room in the Yale Business School library called the Wedge Room. I never heard from lucky Toby Langerfeld again.

THE HUMAN RESOURCE

"Mr. Heinrich would like to see you in his office," Peter's secretary said.

"Now?"

"I think so. His assistant just called while you were on the phone."

"I'll go right up. Tell this Jones he can make another appointment if he can't wait."

Peter Flint, after a year in the personnel department—for unknown reasons suddenly renamed human resources—knew that it was advisable to jump if Heinrich gave an order. Heinrich had maintained his Argentine ways in New York, and those ways demanded instant action. Peter wondered why Argentina, with businessmen like Heinrich, hadn't achieved world-class economic status.

Emilio Heinrich owned and ran the largest Star bottler in South America. Star, of course, was one of the biggest soft drinks in that part of the world. He had been a client, a very successful client, of Dobbs & Johnson Advertising for twenty years, twice threatening to switch agencies if D&J failed to create a sizzling campaign that met with his approval. Both times, D&J met the challenge. And then they came up with one of the most "creative" ideas in the history of advertising agencies. They offered Heinrich the presidency of the New York office. It was impossible to find any other client who had become president of his advertising agency. Emilio Heinrich, aged fifty-five, married, and with five children, was a unique marketing man.

Peter Flint was the youngest of three men and four women in the human resources department. The department's director thought that his youth (twenty-nine, single, nice-enough looking) made him ideal for hiring—among his other duties—the young men and women for the mail room, the first step on the long march toward the agency's hierarchy. No promises of advancement were made to the newcomers. Each young person was advised to learn what he could on the floors where he distributed the mail. Each had to learn how the business operated by wheedling information from writers, artists, account executives, secretaries, whomever they could charmingly exploit for their own ends. The agency had no formal training program.

Peter Flint felt paternal toward these kids, who were only a few years younger than he was. He urged them to be efficient, neat, respectful, eager, and any other scoutlike quality they could think of.

No other mail-room young man was more scoutish than Dan FitzSimmons. And it paid off. Not just one, but two groups wanted him to join them as an assistant account executive. Peter Flint decided the young man should spend two more months in the mail room and then make the switch right after the first of the year. By then young Dan could decide which group to join. And besides, human resources needed time to find a mail-room replacement.

One account director discussing young FitzSimmons told Peter, "He's got a brain, not just a head on his shoulders. Wish he didn't have that damned Southern accent. It might bother one of my clients. He should work on it."

Another account director said, "You know Northern Food has a woman CEO. Also a woman ad director. I think your FitzSimmons could get into bed with one of them, or both. If he were a couple inches taller, it would be a sure thing. I know what those bitches like."

The first account director said, "He's an ambitious little bastard. Has my whole group eating out of his hand. They all want him to join. Especially my queer one, whose name shall never pass my lips."

The other said, "Remember Terry Douglas? Big-shot account exec? Always wore a blazer, double-breasted. Remember when he lost the Crown Builders account? Completely left the business. Didn't even check for a job with other agencies. They say he had a nervous breakdown. A guy I know thinks he spotted him in Denver. Cashier at a 7-Eleven. As they say, 'how the mighty etc.' Looked like an old man. But I guess he'd be only forty, right?"

And then came the call from President Emilio Heinrich's office.

The Argentine's secretary whispered, "Good luck," and motioned Peter to go right in.

"Good morning, sir," said Peter Flint.

"Yes, good morning." Heinrich glanced up and went on reading something on his desk. He kept Peter Flint standing there a good thirty seconds. Then he took off his glasses and stood up.

"I suppose you know this Dan FitzSimmons boy. In the mail room?"

"Yes indeed, sir."

"He must leave. You must fire him."

"What has he done?"

"He hasn't 'done' anything. His father runs Sun Soft Drinks in Jacksonville. I absolutely cannot have that boy snooping around this agency. Star would be horrified. In fact, I am horrified."

"Sun Soft competes with Star? I didn't realize—"

"Of course it does. And they're expanding. Someday a real threat."

"But I—"

"No, no, no! I don't have time to argue. He goes! And one more thing. Do not tell him why he's being fired. Just tell him to leave. Right?"

"That's very hard, sir."

"Yeah, yeah. Life is hard. Just don't tell him. Anything else?"

Peter Flint said, "No, sir. I guess I understand."

"That's nice. Thanks for coming up." And Emilio Heinrich turned back to his desk.

From his own office, Peter Flint phoned the mail room. Yes, Dan happened to be there. He'd be right up.

"Sit," Peter Flint said to Dan. The young man took a chair in front of Peter's desk.

"What's up?" Dan said.

"You have to leave the agency, I'm sorry to say."

"Leave? You mean I'm fired?"

"You can call it that."

After a few seconds staring, paralyzed, Dan stood up. "No! Why the hell? What have I done?" His face was bright red.

"It's nothing you've done, I swear."

"Then why? Why the fuck?"

Peter hated himself and what he was doing. The young man was taking this harder than expected. Peter thought he might break out into sobbing hysterics. But wouldn't that be normal? People didn't get fired for no reason, even in the ad game.

Tears were streaming down Dan's face. "What am I supposed to tell people? What'll I tell my father? Fired for no reason! Oh, you bastard! You fucking bastard!"

Peter gritted his teeth. "I'm sorry. Believe me. You better get going now."

Dan stood stock-still for a minute. Then he sorrowfully shook his head, as if to say, "You poor specimen of a man." He made no effort to wipe the tears off his crimson face.

**

It was two days later that word reached the Human Resources Department that Dan FitzSimmons was in Lenox Hill hospital. Attempted suicide. They'd pumped out his stomach. He'd live. No aftereffects expected.

Peter Flint immediately taxied up to the hospital.

"Yes, he can see visitors. Are you a member of the family?"

"No. His employer."

"That's fine. Go in."

When Dan saw who it was, he pulled himself up on the pillows. "Well, well. I suppose you're here to explain why you fired me. Frankly, I don't give a shit."

"It looks like you gave a shit yesterday. But no matter. I just wanted to tell you something. That's why I came. I've handed in my resignation. I'll be gone in two weeks."

"Because of what you did to me? Gee, I'm touched."

"Well, mainly because of you. I'm just not cut out for that job. Not too fond of working for an Argentine either. And if you ever need a letter of recommendation"—he pulled out of his pocket a slip of paper bearing his home address—"I'll be glad to write one."

After a second, Dan said, "I just don't get it."

"Maybe someday we can have a drink together."

"Yeah. Maybe."

There was nothing more to say. Peter Flint nodded good-bye. Dan FitzSimmons nodded back.

MANUEL, FRIEND

I walked Manuel across the living room to the front door, my hand on his shoulder.

"I hope the trip isn't too hard," I said.

"Well, thanks."

But I knew the trip would be terribly hard. It was hard beyond imagination already, and it hadn't even begun.

"Let's keep in touch," I said. "A letter now and then, OK? And don't forget a Christmas card. I like Christmas cards."

"Sure. You write me too. You have my address. Mexico City?"

"Indeed I do. Maybe you'll have a letter waiting for you when you get home."

"I haven't been home for four years. Four and a half."

"Really? Four years? Yeah, I guess it is. Sorry it has to end."

"Me too."

We shook hands.

Manuel was in his early forties, and I was almost twice his age. My wife, may she rest in peace, and I never had any children. And the more I think about it, the more I guess you could call Manuel a replacement for the son we never had. For a couple of years after she passed, I couldn't quite get my bearings. Wanted to stay home. Didn't mind rattling around in the house all by myself—a damned big house, by the way, for one person, right on the bluff overlooking the ocean, one of the finest locations on Long Island.

My doctor got me introduced to Manuel, sort of indirectly. I've gone for annual check-ups for years. A couple of years ago, quite a while after Mary died, he said I would waste away if I didn't get out more, make some new friends, go to a movie once in a while. Sitting in front of a TV set, he said, didn't give you the lift a crowd at the movies did. But it isn't easy making friends when you're getting older. Face it, your old friends have pretty much disappeared. People are nice to you, but they aren't too inclined to have you for supper. Or ask you to a concert. Or the movies.

Believe it or not, Manuel rang my doorbell. That was the first time we met. He wanted to mow my lawn. He was obviously Hispanic, dark skinned, coal black hair, big dark eyes, and gleaming white teeth. A little under six feet tall. I think when we first met he was just under forty.

The town, Hampton Shores, had been invaded, as some people put it, by Hispanic immigrants. Many years ago, we had loads of Southern blacks coming through to harvest potatoes, but they moved on after a month or so. The locals could never have handled the harvest without their help. So of course, they were more than welcome. But the current army of Hispanic invaders shows no sign of leaving. And instead of being welcomed, they are pretty much despised. Supposedly, they take jobs away from local people, but the local people don't want and won't take the low-paying jobs the Hispanics take. I must admit they're not a pretty sight standing on the corner down by Stop & Shop waiting to be hired. Twenty or thirty of them every morning. Pretty scruffy looking. Unhappy-looking bunch. Just the men. You never see the women. I think the women get a lot of the housekeeping jobs. I've heard that three or four families live together in the same house and probably a pretty crummy house at that. Lucky if they have more than one bathroom. I hear that at night, one of the churches keeps mattresses laid out in the basement for the ones that don't have a roof over their heads.

Manuel was one of the lucky ones. His brother came to Hampton Shores at least eight years ago, before the major invasion, and started up a grounds-keeping business. Mowing lawns, cleaning up gardens, planting hedges—we're very big on hedges around here. When Manuel arrived, he moved in with that brother, Fidel, and, of course, went to work for him. They have a neat little house down on Atkins Road and a couple of pickup trucks to haul their lawn mowers and other equipment. Manuel tells me they have over fifty customers. In the winter, most of them want Manuel and Fidel to plow them out after snowstorms too, so they have some income even in January and February. Fidel usually goes home to Mexico for Christmas.

"It was my wife's idea," Manuel told me soon after he started the weekly mowing of my lawn. "He was only fifteen," he said, referring to his son Tomas. "I thought he was too young, but she really wanted him to come with me. Maybe to make sure I didn't find another woman. Very suspicious, my wife." He laughed.

"Did Tomas want to come?"

"Yes. A big adventure. And he spoke English pretty good. From school. Better than me. I'm still pretty bad, but he knows like lots of words."

"In high school here? Down at Hampton Shores High?"

"Started as a freshman. But now a senior."

I had seen Tomas occasionally when he was helping Manuel around the property. A nice-looking boy. But we had never actually met. He never came into the house with his father. Manuel happened to know how to play Russian bank, a game I used to play many a night with Mary. One afternoon when Manuel was finishing up, I asked him if he wanted to play a couple of rounds, and he thought it would be great. As usual, I had a scotch and soda, not very strong.

"I don't drink," Manuel said. "I had a friend got sent back to Mexico for drinking too much. I never did like to drink. I make sure Tomas doesn't drink either."

It was a hot July evening, and Manuel had a couple of glasses of iced tea. He concentrated on the card game. It's a sort of double solitaire. No need to talk, so he could relax. And that's how our friendship began, over a scotch, an iced tea, and two decks of cards.

The second summer that I knew Manuel, his son got into trouble. Way over the speed limit in a borrowed car and without a driver's license.

"I try to be strict," Manuel said. "But I work until late, and he has lots of friends."

"Have you met any of them?"

"One or two. Girls too. Hampton girls. The Mexican girls don't get involved. It's like that at home too. The girls don't run around if you know what I mean. But these girls are OK. The boys too. I don't think they study much. They all have cars. Lots of rich kids. They don't work as much as Tomas. But I'm glad they are friends with him. It's not easy to make friends."

"How is he reacting to being arrested?"

"He's very sorry. I told him he'd have to come home right after school every day. But there's something else."

I could tell Manuel had something very serious on his mind.

"There's a big fine. Six hundred dollars. I just don't have six hundred dollars all at one time."

"Wow," I said. "That's nasty. When is it due?"

"Next Wednesday," Manuel said. "He's got to go to court." He took a long drink of iced tea. "Can you loan it to me? I can pay you back pretty fast. I send money to my wife. I just won't send it for a while."

It's hard when a friend asks for a loan. You've been raised believing that loaning to a friend is a sure way to lose a friend. But in my whole lifetime, I don't think anyone asked me to loan him more than the cost of a beer. I hesitated.

"I promise to pay it fast," Manuel said.

So I agreed, confident that he'd pay me back.

The court appearance was painful. The judge was from a Hampton family whose roots went back two hundred years. No apparent emotion, certainly not friendly. Only a few onlookers were in the courtroom, but they somehow made it clear that, if asked, they would not recommend mercy for one of the Mexican migrants. Certainly not a teenager, a scruffy male, probably a car thief despite the car owner's swearing he loaned it to Tomas. When Manuel came forward with the six hundred dollars in cash, the onlookers probably thought he'd stolen it. To them he looked dark and dangerous. To me he looked like a father in distress.

In less than a month, Manuel paid me back in full. Plus a bottle of good scotch, which, I must admit, I never expected.

Our card playing became a rather steady ritual. Since during the summer he always mowed for me on Wednesdays, he continued coming by on Wednesdays in the fall and winter, long after any mowing was necessary. Of course, we played cards, but every couple of weeks, he'd bring in a load of wood for the fireplace or swab down my car if it was covered with autumn mud. And I'd insist he take ten dollars or twenty. It was rather like an allowance for a son.

"Tomas has got a girlfriend," Manuel said one evening. "He brought her home to meet me and Fidel."

"Mexican?" I asked.

"No. Local girl. Named Clarkson. Jennie Clarkson. Do you know them?"

"Afraid not."

"She says her father drives the bus. Montauk to Riverhead and back. Six days a week. She says it makes him very tired. Very nervous."

"I should think it would drive him mad," I said. "Keeping on schedule, dealing with idiot passengers, getting everybody to pay."

"The girl looks after him. Her mother's dead."

"So she's pretty responsible. Not a flibbertigibbet."

"What is that?"

"Not important. Local expression."

"I think she's good. I don't know what my wife will think."

"Don't tell me they're serious. Both still in high school?"

"Both seniors. I won't let him get married, don't worry. Maybe when he's twenty-one."

Thanksgiving and Christmas came and went that year, and spring brought the amazing cherry blossoms, the forsythia, and daffodils.

When Manuel arrived for our regular Wednesday game of cards one evening in May, he looked grim.

"What's up?" I asked.

"Very bad," he said. "Tomas has got that girl pregnant. Jennie Clarkson."

"Jesus!" I said.

"She's a Catholic. No abortion."

"So she wants to get married?"

"Maybe. I don't know. I was so mad I didn't ask many questions."

"Are we sure it was Tomas?"

"He says it was, and so does she."

"God, I'm sorry. What a pain!"

And the next day, the way I understand it, Jennie Clarkson's father waited outside the high school and shot Tomas with a rifle. Shot from his car. Hit the boy right in the forehead. Killed him instantly. All the kids kept pouring out of the building. School was just letting out. They say there was general hysteria.

I'll be curious to see how Mr. Clarkson survives the trial for murder. I'm sorry to say it will be almost impossible to find a jury that will convict him, not when a Mexican kid has got a local girl pregnant. Clarkson's only daughter, only child. I can't remember any other Mexicans involved in a serious crime out here, but I bet the local jury will decide Mr. Clarkson was temporarily insane, or Tomas had a criminal record and was dangerous, or . . . well, it will just end up with some sort of slap on the wrist.

The last time I saw Manuel, poor guy, he had been granted custody of his son's body, and he was taking him home to Mexico. He had tried to be strict, but he couldn't spend every waking minute checking up on the boy. Anyway, Tomas was by no means a bad boy. But his death completely poisoned the whole American experience for Manuel. And Jennie Clarkson's pregnancy was no propaganda victory for the migrant Mexicans.

That evening when he was leaving for the last time, he said, "We have been good friends, haven't we?"

"The best," I said. "And you play damned good Russian bank."

"Not many of my people have friends here. You know that, don't you?"

"I suppose you're right."

"I'm sorry I have to leave. But you and I, we've been friends, haven't we?"

"Absolutely."

Then he said, "You have had no son?"

"Afraid not."

"But you can think."

"Do you mean *imagine*? Oh God, yes, I can imagine."

He nodded and headed down the driveway to his pickup truck.

A MINOR FAMILY FRAUD

"I hope you like the idea," she said.

"She's your aunt. It's up to you," he said.

"But I'm doing it for our daughter, not for myself."

"I know. But it still seems a little dishonest."

"It isn't. Not for a minute. I'll tell her why we want it, and that'll be the truth."

"She's seventy-six," he said. "It's sort of like stealing candy from a baby."

"The way I see it," she said, "it's more like stealing candy *for* a baby."

"I'll go along with it, whatever you decide."

Her Aunt Ada lived three hundred miles away, so they would have to stay overnight with her. At least they wouldn't have to pay for a motel. And Ada would feed them. She always said, and seemed to mean it, that they were her favorite niece and nephew-in-law. Probably she said that to all her relatives. She had no children of her own, but like many single women, she had inherited the bulk of her parents' estate. Parents used to think that single women needed all the help they could get to survive in the modern world.

"We'll have to say that Bonnie is going to be a real virtuoso," she said.

"That's no lie," he said.

"What? That we'll have to say it? Or Bonnie's going to be a star?"

"Well, you're going to handle it. I'm not good at this sort of shit. I'm going to be totally quiet. Understood?"

"No," she said. "That is not understood. You've got to back me up. Everybody says Bonnie is a prodigy. A twelve-year-old prodigy. There's no lie involved. What about that applause at the Lions convention? That awful old wreck she plays on doesn't help, but she still manages to put it over. Whatever she plays, they love. Imagine what would happen if—"

"She's damned cute on stage. I think that's part of it."

"So? Some of those women in New York are damned cute too, and it doesn't hurt their careers, not one bit."

Aunt Ada lived in Ardsley, outside of Philadelphia. Her four-bedroom house was on two acres. Her car was a three-year-old Cadillac. She had only one noticeable failing. (A cardinal sin, a nephew in Chicago said, but he had only a Christmas-card closeness to her.) Her failing was her things. Her silver-framed photo portraits of all her relatives, dead and alive. Her sterling tableware, inherited from her parents, who inherited it from her maternal grandmother. Her perfectly placed, antique (but comfortable) furniture, spotlessly upholstered in soft greens and ivories, colors matched by the wall-to-wall carpeting.

Twenty years ago, she gave an occasional tea for the Presbyterian ladies but did no entertaining since her bout with cancer (in total remission, the doctors said). She once, long ago, even gave a garden party, which resulted in having to resod the garden lawn and replace two crystal goblets. These days, one of her neighbors might come by for a predinner whiskey, or Ada might walk down the street for lunch with the district attorney's wife, but her entertaining days were over. Of course, she loved seeing her family whenever they chose to drop by. But they paid her very few visits.

Since the family children were not very warmly welcomed while they were still too young to understand the heartbreak of a broken glass or a mud-stained carpet, they lost, as they grew older, whatever desire they might have had to visit Aunt Ada. They could hardly remember her or her house.

"Has she got all her marbles?" he asked, pulling into her gravel driveway.

"As far as I know. I think so. She seemed glad to hear we were coming. Mom was perfect right up to the day she died. I should think Ada will be the same."

Since they were two hours later than they planned, Ada had given up sitting by the front window. She was startled by the doorbell. For a moment, she could not imagine who it could be. Then, of course, she remembered.

"Come in, come in," she said. "Oh, how lovely to see you both. It's been too long, hasn't it?"

"Much, much too long," her niece said, giving her a peck on the cheek.

"You're looking great," he said. "Haven't changed a bit."

"Haven't I? What a nice thing to hear. Why don't you just put that suitcase at the bottom of the stairs. I bet you're exhausted. It must have taken forever in this traffic. What about a cup of tea? Or a drink? Wouldn't you like a drink?"

"We got off to a late start," he said, "so we stopped for lunch. We don't need a thing, thanks. I'll take this upstairs. You girls get caught up."

"He's a sweetie, isn't he," Ada said. "I haven't been called a girl for a hundred years. I love it."

She motioned her niece to the couch. She sat in an easy chair. "It's really lovely to see you, dear," she said. "I hope you're not going to run off until the weekend."

"Well, we'll see," said her niece. "It's so beautiful here I'd like to stay forever."

She glanced at the Steinway, a parlor grand, polished to ebony perfection. It's lid was down, as always, but there was nothing on it, not even flowers. It looked somehow naked.

"What are you staring at, dear? Have I moved the piano?"

"Maybe. It just looks different. Maybe it's the light."

"Oh, it must be the light. I can't remember moving it. Or did I? Do you think I did?"

She wished her husband would come back downstairs. She was getting angrier at him every second. "I just wish you could hear our Bonnie play. She's really good even if I am her mother."

"Piano, is it?" said Ada.

"Oh, no. Well yes, at the start it was piano. You're right. She was very good. Very. But now it's violin. They say she could go all the way to the top."

"I wish I could hear her. Someday maybe. What is she, eight or nine?"

"Our Bonnie's a big girl now. Twelve. And you'd think she was twenty. Very poised."

Ada shook her head. "This all reminds me of something, but I can't remember what. It's awful getting old."

"It reminds you of something? What reminds you of something?"

"Something you said, I guess. That happens to me all the time. I think of something one minute and can't remember it the next. It's a real burden."

"It wasn't the violin, was it? The one you always had on the piano? The piano looks sort of bare without it."

"Oh, of course. It was always right there, wasn't it? With its old case. It was so old."

"I hope you put it somewhere safe. I bet it's pretty valuable."

"This lovely man came to see me. Do you remember my friend, Florence Cartwright from Boston? She came to your wedding with me. She wrote me this letter about Mr. Smythe. He's the one that came to see me. Only a week or two ago, maybe a month. I think he loved everything in the house. I've never had a real antique dealer come by. He was so complimentary. Made me feel like a real princess. He loved that portrait of your grandfather—no, your great-grandfather—he wanted to buy it. Can you believe it? I told him no of course. I'm sure you'll want it someday. It hung over the fireplace in our house in Baltimore. Mother thought it was too big for that mantle, but Dad wanted it to stay. Dad always got his way. Mother was smarter I've always thought, but Dad was a lawyer, so he always won. You don't remember my father, do you? Such a wonderful man. And handsome. He looked grand in his uniform. Mother had a picture of him, thank the Lord. War is terrible, isn't it?"

"It certainly is. Just terrible." Her eyes had searched every shelf, every surface, in the room. "Did you sell the antique dealer anything? I don't suppose so. Your things are just too lovely to sell to an antique dealer."

"Well, believe it or not I seem to remember selling him something, whatever it was. He'd still be here if I hadn't agreed. He was very persistent but very nice. Florence would never have recommended him if he was, oh I don't know, 'coarse,' you know." She laughed. "Between you and me, he could have stayed forever as far as I was concerned. I was old enough to be his mother, but he had a very mature way of dealing with things. Very attractive in his way, you know. For a New Yorker."

"I just can't imagine what you'd sell." She was ready to curse her husband if he failed to come down those stairs in the next five seconds. Then Aunt Ada would know what *coarse* sounded like.

"Now let me guess what you might have sold him."

"I just can't remember a thing."

"I'm sure you wouldn't dream of selling him Grandpa's old violin."

"It was so battered, wasn't it? The case, I mean. All bruised and torn. I wouldn't have wanted to be seen in public with that old thing."

"But the violin itself? It was as old as the case, wasn't it?"

"Oh, much, much older. Mr. Smythe just loved it. I remember. He said it would need repairs, but he was willing to see to it. He had some funny name for it. Italian, I think. I've never been any good at foreign languages, have you? It reminded me of Don Ameche, I remember. I can remember the strangest things. Or was it the Amalfi coast, where my parents went on their honeymoon? Have you been to Italy, dear? It's so nice. Maybe you and your husband would like to come with me someday. Wouldn't that be nice? The three of us doing Italy. I'd love to visit Amalfi."

If she made any sort of comment other than a big smile, she might be sending a trip to Italy down the tubes. Or worse, she might say something "coarse" about itinerant swindlers who fed like vampires off innocent old women. Innocent and ignorant. Or ask how much the bastard had paid for that violin, which was intended to turn her Bonnie into a female Itzak Perlman.

"You know, dear," said Ada, "come to think of it, I think that old violin will more than pay for a trip to Italy. I never thought of it that way. But it sounds good to me. Maybe there's even enough for your daughter. What's her name?"

"Bonnie." Big smile.

"Of course. Bonnie. Do you think she'd like to go with us? Or is she too young? What did you say she was? Eight or nine?"

"A little older than that. Just a little."

"I do want to talk it over with your husband. I bet he makes all the decisions in your family, doesn't he? My father did. He was a lawyer. Wait 'till you see the men in Italy. Oh my lord, are they ever handsome. We all act as if we don't like being pinched, but it's really not all that bad. Not at all."

"I'd better go see what's happened to my husband. You know we'll have to be on the road before dark, or we'll never get home."

"Dark? Tonight? You're not leaving tonight?"

"Now, Aunt Ada. You know I said we'd just drop by for a minute."

"But the suitcase."

"Just what we needed driving down. Not for overnight. I never said overnight."

"Of course you didn't. What's gotten into me?"

"Well, we all misunderstand things now and then."

"But I would like to hear Bonnie play. Do you think I'll ever hear her play? It's the violin, isn't it?"

"Oh, I can't wait for you to hear her play. I just can't wait."

DOOZY

"Well," she said, "I'll have a couple of extra dollars, now that he's dead. I guess that's one way of looking at it. Always look for the silver lining, I say."

My Aunt Janet was talking about her dog Doozy, a cross between a collie and a lab, sand colored, she said, and I gathered about forty pounds. He must have been a wonderful companion, but it was my bad luck never to have met him. She kept me up to date on his doings, though, whenever we talked on the phone. She had a snug cottage in the Connecticut woods, and I lived and worked in Manhattan. I tried to visit her every eight or ten weeks. She was my mother's sister. Never married.

I followed her out into the garden behind the house. The May grass was just filling in after a typically frigid winter. She wanted to show me where she'd buried her "best friend."

She pointed to a spot in front of a large azalea.

"You see the outline?" She pointed at the ground. "I got out my trusty old edger. I didn't dig too deep."

I'm not sure I actually saw the grave's outline, but I nodded respectfully.

"I cut the sods up real carefully so I could lay them back. Pretty good job, right?"

"Gosh, yes," I said. "When the grass grows a bit more, there won't be a trace."

"That's what I hoped for." She took my arm and headed back to the kitchen door.

She had installed a dog-port years ago. It was bigger than any I'd seen elsewhere, but Doozy was no toy poodle. Still, it looked like he'd have to squeeze a little to get through.

"You know," she said, "Some of my friends called him a feral dog. For the longest time, I thought that was an insult, but you know what it means?

139

It means he was a dog who'd gone wild. Reverted to wolf. Lived off the land. Well, of course, he wasn't feral at all. He was just adventurous. Loved to hang out in the woods. Sort of a doggy Thoreau."

"But he always came home for supper," I said. Frankly, I didn't remember his coming in even though I'd been visiting pretty much his whole lifetime.

"Well, yes. But I think he was shy. Know what I mean? Either hid from strangers or scared the devil out of them. He had a bark you could hear in Miami. You heard him, didn't you?"

"Not that I remember. Isn't that funny?"

"He scared Willy, our postman, so bad he wouldn't even come in the driveway. Left the mail all bundled up just by the curb. Doozy was proud of that. He'd listen for Willy, bark his head off, and then run out to the street and bring the mail in. Lay it at my feet and wait to get a cracker. Maybe I spoiled him a little."

"I can't say I ever heard the bark, but I can imagine just what it was like."

"And you know," she said, "one time he brought in a baby robin that had fallen out of its nest. Carried it so gently there was hardly a bit of down out of place. Couldn't have been more than a couple days old. You know the way cats bring in mice or chipmunks? That's what he did with that robin. I couldn't have carried it more carefully myself. Gentle as could be."

I said, "That's a new one. I never heard of a dog doing that sort of thing. Is that very common?"

"Oh no, I should say not. Not for a collie. I guess bird dogs do it all the time. And when I'd take him on a leash, go for a walk, he would take the middle of the leash in his mouth, almost as if he was leading me. We were awfully good friends."

"How old was he?"

"Seventeen," she said. "I bought him for myself on my sixtieth birthday. He was just eight weeks old. But right from the start, golly could that boy eat. A half can of Alpo and two handfuls of nuggets every night. And I suspect he caught a rabbit now and then for dessert. Sometimes he wouldn't come in until I'd gone to bed. But his dinner was always gone in the morning. And his water dish was empty."

"So, as you say, now you'll have a couple of extra bucks. No more Alpo."

"Well, like I told Louise Spaulding, when I heard those brakes screeching out in the road, I knew just what had happened. I couldn't go through that again. I swear I couldn't. Nobody around to help. The driver left. Doozy dead as a doornail. I could hardly pull him up on the sidewalk, crying my eyes out, acting like a damn fool over a dead dog. Never another dog for me, thank you. But that was a week ago. I got over it."

"Awful," I said. "So sorry."

She stood up. "Tea time," she announced. "That's what we old Connecticut ladies do these days. Makes the afternoon go by a little faster. Now you just sit still. It won't take a minute."

But I got up and looked at all the familiar things in the room. I noticed something on the mantle. It was a brand-new leather dog collar, so new it still smelled leathery as if it were barely out of the box. It had certainly never spent a night in the woods.

Good God, what an imagination she had. She probably grew to believe every word herself. And brought in "exhibits" to prove it.

Of course, the bright unscratched nameplate said Doozy.

THE CHEETAH UNDER THE CHAIR

We were delighted here at *Bath & Den* to receive the invitation from Doreen Fitz-Frawley to visit her new home in Greenwich Village. For those readers of *B&D* who may not be familiar with Fitz-Frawley's work, let's just say that she is most famous for her interiors at the Time-Life condos, her stage sets for *Boys Aloft* (now on the road, being applauded in eighteen American cities), and the stunning new Primates' World at the Bronx Zoo. She is still on the short list to rearticulate Shea Stadium and has become a dedicated evangelical Christian while bidding on the expansion of California's Crystal Cathedral.

We expected to find her apartment (she calls it "Fitz's Flat," in deference to her six-week course at London's Interiors Institute) severely formal and perhaps nothing short of monochromatic—she has used a surprising beige throughout her work at Time-Warner, and bright magenta highlights caught the eye at Primates' World.

But we were wrong. With a self-effacing bow to classic Parisian decor, she has chosen deep and rich greens and purples for the first floor, and striking carnelian and off-aquas for the bedrooms. The master bedroom is, of course, midnight black, emphasizing the leather flooring, created, she confesses, from four dozen wrestling mats intended for New England schools (she grew up, appropriately, in South Boston), not to mention the bed itself, consisting of three massage tables on wheels, cleverly locked together but easily separated. "Nobody these days wants to stay too close after dalliance," she insists, slapping her Vegas cowboy boot with a stainless-steel-tipped Glastonbury riding crop.

The afternoon we were invited for an interview and a look-see, we noticed that the marble steps leading up to her nineteenth-century walnut front door were highly polished and glazed, reminiscent of interior stairs at the Vatican—a nice touch, we thought, for impressionable visitors of any denomination. When we rang the doorbell, which was cleverly concealed in a stuffed rabbit's head, the racket inside, ricocheting around those elderly walls, was startling. In fact, this reporter thought for a moment an ambulance was roaring down the quaint little alley that Fitz-Frawley has renamed Jean Genet Close. But the rabbit ears stopped waving, signaling that the door would soon be opened.

Since our readers are interested exclusively in furniture, art, flower arranging and jewelry (so says our research department), I won't dwell on the fine male creature, minimally dressed, who answered the door. I will only paraphrase that grand old Chrysler commercial, "If you can find a better body, buy it!"

Fitz-Frawley couldn't have been more gracious. Exquisite demitasse cups with deepest "coffee extraordinaire" awaited us in the drawing room where I was seated on a wonderfully comfortable chaise, wide enough for a Marlon Brando or Orson Welles. Soon after settling in, I sensed a warm, regular breeze on my ankles. Despite reservations, I mentioned it to my hostess, assuming it was one of her air-conditioning triumphs, like those that had won her the assignment at Time-Warner.

With a rather condescending smile she said, "Ah, I'm so sorry. I had no idea Zimbabwe was up from below. But you know how cheetahs love to explore. Under that chaise is one of his favorite hiding places. He's not bothering you, is he?"

"Of course not," I said. But I couldn't help flouting every convention and pulled my legs up under me, yoga fashion. In deference to the chair's damask upholstery, I left my shoes on the floor. One of them instantly disappeared under the chair. I can thankfully report that my foot wasn't still in it. The gentle feline wheeze I had first heard turned into a slobbering, wet chewing. Fitz-Frawley didn't seem to notice.

I made all the appropriate clucking sounds as my hostess explained the provenance of various objects in the room. A mahogany table was from the Winter Palace in St. Petersburg. A Ming-period reproduction had been found on the sidewalk at the corner of Greenwich Avenue and Mulberry. The carpet, which was a pale pinkish ivory streaked with purple rivulets reminded me, I must admit, of my Aunt Edith's varicose veins. Of course I kept that reminiscence to myself.

Before ascending to the master bedroom (mistress bedroom?) I've already described, I asked to use the facilities. I was pointed toward a door off the entrance hall. The light flicked on as I opened the door revealing, to my horror, a huge reptile, a man-eating boa constrictor as far as I know, coiled in the bathtub, staring at me with piercing black eyes that struck me as urgently hungry.

"Pay no attention to Rudy Giuliani," Fitz-Frawley called through the door. "He's had his eight gerbils, so I don't think he'll want anything more. But I may be wrong. Just don't tease him."

Thanks to an overactive bladder, I was quickly able to "do my duty," and escaped the bathroom without incident. I almost asked my hostess the provenance of Rudy. But being neither familiar with the policies of the Bronx Zoo nor the Amazon jungle, I realized I had not the slightest curiosity about Rudy's native land.

After my tour of the house, Fitz-Frawley, without even offering to loan me a pair of shoes, summoned the Adonis-like butler—or whatever he was—to see me out. As I stepped shoeless through the door, he whispered, "Please, please, please notify the police. They've got to get me out of here! Please!"

Of course, he made a fine addition to her zoological collection and didn't appear underfed, and I knew my job would be only a memory if I even dreamt of turning her in to the police. So I put the whole thing behind me, made my way in stocking-feet to the subway, and hastened to my next assignment, Itzak Perlman.

Printed in the United States
104788LV00007B/31'1/A

9 781425 787776